Not So Great Dictator

Making Wales Great Again

Articles written for the Eye eMagazine

https://the-eye.wales

Published by
Llyfrau Cambria Books, Wales, United Kingdom.
Cambria Books is a division of
Cambria Publishing.
Discover our other books at: www.cambriabooks.co.uk

Contents

Introduction

As I write this it is early 2019 with the nation staring down the barrel of a hard Brexit. A year and a half ago I was approached by The Eye to write a column and to be honest, I had no idea where I would go with it. From my first story, about farmers blinging up the bailing twine they use to support their trousers, to my latest about Swansea council washing away a £300,000 Banksy, the fake news format has given me the scope to write anything I want, almost any way I want.

I'm fascinated by fake news and by using real people as fictional characters. I also like the development of these fictional worlds over time. There's fun to be had in the challenge of fitting rapidly changing news events into a narrow world with strict constraints.

Liberace/Donald Trump and Nigel Farage sharing a static caravan in Fishguard is something which brings global events right down to earth with a bump. The idea of UNESCO awarding world heritage status to a particularly long-standing system of roadworks hopefully makes people less stressed out about their first world problems.

It's been great fun creating fictional worlds out of real events which I suppose is what all writers do. If I'm honest Kim Jong Un paying for Swansea's Tidal Lagoon so he can use it as a Godzilla nursery has been my favorite story line so far but then I love a bit of sci-fi.

I create fantastical worlds populated by extreme characters which perhaps is a reaction to the way the world has descended into chaos in the last 10 years. In a world where truth jumped out of the window a long time ago the phrase 'truth is stranger than fiction' might still be true but if it is, how would we know?

This book is divided up by subject rather than date which will hopefully make the storylines, occasionally fractured though they are, easier to follow. Some of the stories are one off reactions to current affairs and these I have called 'News' although even some of these have a common theme. Others are longer running storylines loosely corresponding with whatever was happening in the news when I wrote them.

The problem these days is that even though Brexit has been dominating the headlines seemingly forever, there are so many insane developments within it and they happen so quickly it's impossible to keep up with the twists and turns. For this reason, I have avoided dealing with it head on but it does crop up obliquely in a few articles.

Luckily there's always someone doing something insane like renaming the Severn bridge 'The Prince of Wales bridge' without asking anyone in Wales what they thought of the idea. Or proposing an actual 'Ring of Iron', the single most hated three words in the History of Wales, be built as an historic monument.

I've had great fun writing these stories and I hope you have fun reading them.

If you do, then by all means let me know on

Twitter: @notsogreatdictator

Facebook: www.facebook.com/NotSoGreatDictator

The News

Twijazzling Furore at the Royal Welsh

A blazing row has erupted at the Royal Welsh show that threatens to eclipse even the now legendary leering sheep scandal at the 2010 Sheeptacular, when a Beulah Speckled Face ram was accused of giving Dave Price's girlfriend funny looks. Dave offered him out but was placated with Scampi Fries and a selection of cheese samplers.

Even worse than that is this year's rapidly escalating Twijazzling scandal. This all stems from a Twijazzling boutique that's set up stall half way up Avenue G and has seen queues forming at 7 in the morning. Sometimes of people. For the uninitiated perhaps I'd better explain what Twijazzling is.

Ever wondered where farmers buy their clothes? Those green corduroy trousers, tweed jackets and flat caps? I can reliably inform you it is at the Royal Welsh Show. Stroll around the show ground and you will see outlets aplenty selling accoutrements from wellies to walking sticks and everything in between. Every item comes in a variety of styles and can be individualised by the stylish farmer about town. Every item that is except for the ubiquitous bailing twine used by all farmers to keep their trousers from falling down when in mixed company.

This indispensable piece of attire has so far been neglected by gentlemen's outfitters and farmers have traditionally been left to fend for themselves, often wearing the same piece of twine for decades. This year however all that has changed and not everyone is happy about it. In the divisively named 'Twine Town' Twijazzling Boutique, stall holder Glynog Ap Glynog is offering a range of designer bailing twine for the discerning young farmer.

Cut to length and hand seared to prevent fraying, each twine is individually crafted out of organic, local fibres using hypo-allergenic dyes and 3D printed with the message of your choice. When our reporter spoke to him, Glynog was more than willing to outline his vision for the future of trouser support technology.

"We use a lot of glitter *as well as natural fibres. The juxtaposition of the traditional and the overtly, you might say ironically, camp visual imagery expresses a new confidence and we find young farmers want the ability to strut. The* peacock can be just as at home amongst *silage as a celebrity gala. We've sold three quarters of a ton this week and have had to send to Beijing for more glitter".*

Gruffydd Thomas of the Llandeilo milk farmers book club was equally forthcoming but in a more critical vein.

"I'm sick *of all these* hipsters, *not one of them's seen a farm. Trampling all over our traditional traditions. The bailing twine belt has been around as long as, well, either belts or bailing twine, I don't know but that's not the point. I've got bailing twine around my waist because I can't be arsed to buy a belt. My father couldn't be* arsed *before me and his father couldn't be* arsed *before him. You've got these young farmers, that don't even need belts spending all this time on that Internet looking for* blinged up *bailing twine, they want their heads read. It'll come to* no good, *you mark my words."*

A spokesman for the Royal Welsh Show Ground said *"Stall holders are allowed to sell anything that doesn't contravene the laws of England and Wales. To be honest Gruffydd is always* banging on *about something so we tend not to listen anymore".*

The designer bailing twine industry is worth an estimated £5.3 million annually to the Welsh economy and plans to expand into Devon, Cornwall and Shoreditch have been enthusiastically welcomed although not by Gryffudd Thomas who has now gone on hunger strike *"until they at least take the glitter out".*

15,000 sheep a day disappearing up Ken Skates' Massive Ring

Once again Wales is leading the world with its world leading technology and the English are gutted. The Eye Magazine can exclusively reveal the hidden, secret, clandestine, classified, under cover and downright shifty truth about Ken Skates and his much-abused ring of iron. A close examination of the publicity shots and a direct message from someone who, for reasons of laziness, I shall refer to as 'Deep Throat' leads to the inevitable conclusion that it is in fact a sheep Stargate.

With Brexit rapidly approaching Welsh ministers are looking further afield for export opportunities and the Andromeda Galaxy has been provisionally identified as an area usefully devoid of 'Destination Control' red tape. Concerned about the uncertain future of Welsh exports, Ken Skates AM Cabinet Secretary for Economy and Infrastructure set his officials the task of finding territories without barriers to trade. They immediately identified most of Wales as being tariff free, the exception being Pontcanna which has a £5million flat import duty on anything not labelled 'Home Made' including ironically, mobile homes.

After looking at the data Mr. Skates decided selling things in Wales wasn't technically exporting so issued instructions to widen the scope of the research. Minutes later the algorithms threw up the Andromeda galaxy as the nearest suitable market and the adventure began.

Luckily the Assembly had a Stargate, left over from when First Minister The Rt Hon Carwyn Jones AM defeated the 'Klatooine Overlords of Menace' by travelling to Ursa Major on an off season day return and slaying their clan leader in a brutal knife attack. He said he'd had a lovely day out but only gave the

Stargate a 2 on TripAdvisor because on the return journey they served his pork scratchings in a plastic wicker basket which he thought was '*too self-consciously retro*'.

For that reason, the Stargate has lain dormant in the bowels of the Assembly ever since which seems fair enough. Having seen it in action though, Mr. Skates was determined to exploit its potential. Once he'd identified the correct funding stream it was simply a case of finding a convincing cover story and a suitable location.

For unknown reasons anything to do with aliens or alien technology has to be kept absolutely secret so telling the press we were about to send our unwanted sheep through an inter-galactic matter transporter was out of the question.

This is when he hit upon the brilliant idea of saying it was a piece of public art celebrating the subjugation of the Welsh people in a relentless campaign of brutality and humiliation by the Norman invaders. Knowing this would enrage the public he rightly assumed nobody except the English Defence League would ever visit it so he would be free to send thousands of sheep a day through it in total secrecy.

The maths of it depended on the labyrinthine nature of agricultural subsidies and a post Brexit promise he'd seen on the side of a bus. According to his calculations all he needed to do was get the sheep out of the country and as long as there were no tariffs the other side, Wales would be in profit. Jane Hutt suggested pushing them off the Menai bridge but it turned out the buggers could swim.

I know some people will say this is just science fiction and there's no way the Welsh government could operate a sheep Stargate to another galaxy. What I say to them is, the truth is over by there.

Ken Skates shakes his booty in your brain

In order to maintain the fiction of his '*Ring of Iron*' being an ill thought out piece of environmental art Ken Skates AM, Cabinet Secretary for Economy and Infrastructure dramatically fired his director of communications this week and replaced her with the recently available Anthony Scaramucci. The plot thickened further when rumours started to circulate that Mr. Skates and Mr. Scaramucci were in fact twin brothers, separated at birth by an evil magician.

This is based on an uncanny physical resemblance and the cold hard fact that in ancient Norwegian Scaramucci means '*one who glides on ice*'. Anti nepotism rules introduced in 2002 as a result of the 'Hutt Hutt' scandal mean that no cabinet member is allowed to hire anyone who's DNA could be mistaken for their own at a crime scene.

The '*Hutt Hutt*' scandal erupted when Leader of the House and Chief Whip Jane Hutt AM cloned herself so she could attend committee meetings and watch Storage Hunters at the same time. She got away with it for three months until eventually she was caught standing on her own shoulders, wearing a massive raincoat, trying to get into an 18 certificate film.

If Mr. Skates and Mr. Scaramucci, or S.S as they have quickly become known in the corridors of power turn out to be twins it will fulfill the prophecy which is said to be a sign of the coming apocalypse. The exact wording of the prophecy is lost in the mists of time but in modern parlance it translates to *"If one is a government minister and the other a recently fired,* foul *mouthed, self-admitted* front stabber *and they shall be twin brothers, the world of man on its axis will turn* no *more and the light of the sun shall* not *bring forth another hopeful dawn"*.

The prophecy aside we have to hand it to Mr. Scaramucci who has set to work with rare enthusiasm and has already changed the name of his department from '*The Department for Economy and Infrastructure*' to '*The Department for Economy and Infrastructure* Sound Machine'. This he believes will give it a more vital and cutting-edge public image. It will also force people to imagine Mr. Skates dancing to the conga rhythms of Dr Beat whenever his name is mentioned on TV.

Ken Skates urges English settlers to Remember Tryweryn in bid to stem controversy

Hoping to placate critics following revelations that officials had discussed beforehand how the controversial 'Ring of Iron' sculpture could be seen as celebrating the suppression of Welsh uprisings, Economy Secretary Ken Skates has launched an initiative designed to boost investment in rural areas.

The scheme will start with a pilot project based around the idea of the Oklahoma Land Rush. English settlers will be allowed to start their engines at the Severn bridge tolls and each will be allotted a quarter section of land just north of the Llyn Celyn reservoir.

The first to reach the area can claim the land free of charge and build whatever they like. The land has already been divided into plots and pre-ploughed to make it easier for newcomers to lay sewage pipes under their static caravans.

In unrelated news, the Channel 4's Grand Designs will be filming a mini-series based in the sunken village of Capel Celyn. The series will feature Hermione and Lancelot Rees-Mogg who plan to restore the old village post office under a geodesic dome built in The Ukraine. The Reese-Moggs have assured local planning officials in Liverpool City Council that their Bauhaus inspired renovation will respect the original character of traditional Welsh building materials whilst at the same time bringing a holistic and sustainable approach to underwater living.

The most expensive aspect of the design will be the 30-metre windscreen wiper they will use to constantly scrape the dome free of raw sewage being dumped on it by the new settlers on the shores of the reservoir above. Presenter Kevin McCloud hailed it as a brave and magnificent contribution to the conversation between domestic architecture and the challenging environment of having way more money than sense.

The advertising campaign for the Land Rush initiative which will see hundreds of English settlers occupying the slopes of the Tryweryn Valley begins on TV in December. Echoing the Tell Sid campaign for the British Gas floatation of the 80s the adverts will feature friendly English villagers from all walks of village life being encouraged to 'Remember Tryweyn'. So they don't forget when they can pick up free land courtesy of the Welsh government.

A Welsh government spokesman said *"The trickle-down effect of wealthy English second homeowners will revitalise the local economy and help develop better relations between the two nations. It is hoped this boost to the rural economy will dispel any lingering questions about whether or not Mr. Skates fully understands the historical context of his department's initiatives."*

After a fifteen-week historical sensitivity training workshop in Milton Keynes, Mr. Skates acknowledges that *"mistakes have been made in the past but what our communities need most is a sense of financial security. Having said that, the historical concerns of local communities are of paramount importance to me and I would never do anything to cause distress."*

Heddlu Lamarr (A masked avenger is born)

Jeffrey Aloysius St John Hambley Cuthbert placed his feet on the edge of his vast oak desk and leaned back in his chair. Having been elected Police and Crime Commissioner for Gwent he knew he'd achieved a great deal since absconding, as an 11-year-old, from St Beyonce's academy for the punishment of minor infringements. He stared out the window and before he knew it a familiar melancholy descend like a slightly green chip in an otherwise perfect fish supper.

He knew the cause of his fug very well. He also knew only one thing would drive it away. For all his prestige and high office, he felt powerless. Day in, day out he faced the same endless barrage of crime statistics. Drugs, murder, people/hamster smuggling, you name it, they did it. He had high hopes when he started. He'd be a man of the people and get them behind the idea of a new kind of police force. Unfortunately, as he kept having to arrest 'the people', they weren't getting behind the idea as much as he'd hoped.

Three months to the day after starting the job he'd had enough. That day would be burned into his soul forever. That day would see him take back the streets. Would see the dawn of a new age; an age of direct action and individual heroism for that was the day he donned the mask and cape of a new force. A new hero would patrol the mean streets of Pontllanfraith and mete out instant justice. By day he would be mild mannered Police and Crime Commissioner Jeff Cuthbert, by night, cross dressing masked avenger Heddlu Lamarr.

The criminals of Gwent would once again know fear and to be honest, a fair degree of confusion. Its citizens would know pride. He vowed he would use his power for good and to defend the weak from tyranny, by whatever means it took. He would not let the criminals win. Every cell in his body cried freedom. He would make mid and south east Wales, great again or die trying. A superhero/heroine was born that day. A legendary warrior on a quest for greater public safety, renewed social cohesion and raw naked vengeance.

And so it begins.

The Swansea Bay Tidal Lagoon and Godzilla

The Swansea Bay Tidal Lagoon proposed development was happening at the same time as the situation with North Korea was getting a bit heated. I thought it would be funny if Swansea council, desperate for money and prestige took on a scheme which would inevitably lead to their own terrible destruction. One of the only long running themes in politics is the rabid short termism engendered by the demands of electoral cycles.

This is an extreme example of that, plus the embarrassing one-upmanship practiced by politicians of all hues if they think the public can be bought with some shiny baubles. Also, Kim Jong Un and Donald Trump's utterances are that insane, their actual words need very little tweaking in order to become beyond ridiculous. It's a potent combination which lends itself easily to parody.

Swansea Bay Tidal Lagoon to be North Korean Godzilla Nursery

Swansea councillors today announced their determination to develop a Tidal Lagoon regardless of any financial decisions made by central government in Westminster.

A number of self-funding options are being looked at including renting it out to the Pembrokeshire Underwater Caravan Society whose dream of a camp site free from BBQs and loud music can finally become a reality.

The preferred option, however, is a Godzilla nursery for colourful tyrant Kim Jong-un. The North Korean government has expressed an interest in developing an elite squad of highly trained Taekwondo Godzillas with which to threaten the United States and assert their dominance across the Sea of Japan. Unfortunately, international sanctions mean they are unable to secure a sufficiently pure supply of Lava Bread with which to wean the pups.

A leaked report from the Enterprise, Development and Regeneration department at the City and County of Swansea shows how far negotiations have advanced. This excerpt, reproduced below under parliamentary privilege, was secured by our reporter at great expense to both his conscience and dignity.

Economic impact

- Large *bundles* of unmarked bills being unloaded in the dead of night from shipping containers on the steps of County Hall.
- Shockingly extravagant spending sprees by North Korean diplomats high on crack, toting machine guns.

- Lava Bread prices sky rocketing, enabling vast *seaweed* based empires to develop, transforming the C.Watts Cockle Rotunda in Swansea Market into a blinged up hipster paradise.

Community benefits

- A Godzilla petting *zoo*.
- Full employment for previously underutilized Godzilla wranglers.
- Cultural exchange opportunities between Swansea and Pyongyang.
- The Godzillas will eat all the underwater *caravan* enthusiasts.

Risks

- Insufficient Lava Bread to satisfy local demand.
- Traffic congestion relating to the Godzilla petting zoo.
- Complete devastation, for generations to come, of Swansea and the surrounding areas by giant, fire breathing, nuclear mutant lizard creatures.

A freedom of Information request has revealed a backdoor channel has been opened up between Pyongyang and the City and County of Swansea Council. Godzilla eggs are currently being stockpiled in the Amazon Fulfilment Centre in Crymlyn Burrows. If funding is secured from Westminster the eggs will simply be transferred to the exotic/killer pets section and discounted on Black Friday.

Cardiff City Council instigates Mothra Breeding Programme in Principality Stadium

Cardiff Council today issued a press release detailing their intention to develop a Mothra breeding program to counteract the Godzilla threat from the Swansea Bay Tidal Lagoon independent finance initiative. The Principality stadium is the perfect incubator and Ministry of Defence funding will supply the £24m needed to balance books at Cardiff Council.

Mothra, (a giant mutant moth-type creature) is widely believed to be the mortal enemy of Godzilla and is number 1,282 on the World Wildlife Fund's endangered species directory.

A spokesman for the council, whose name (Jeff Sarphngywumpts) remains unpronounceable for legal reasons, stated *"The Mothra breeding season fits in perfectly with the current requirements of the Principality Stadium events calendar"*. He added *"Barring unforeseen events we anticipate no more than a dozen or so fatal incidents in the first two weeks and then almost none for a few days. The Mothras are very friendly and mostly not too killy on weekends"*.

Pressed further on the 'killy' aspects of the Mothra life cycle Mr. Sarphngywumpts started complaining about 'Fake News' and said he was *"By far the most persecuted of all the press officers announcing reckless policy decisions"*.

From what we can gather the plan is to house the Mothras in the Principality Stadium until they are mature enough to engage in a world-shattering conflict with giant sea dwelling, fire breathing, nuclear mutant lizard creatures. In anticipation of the breeding program the stadium owners have replaced the standard floodlights with one giant light bulb in the middle of the ceiling. 'To make them feel at home'.

The issue of what to do with the Mothras when the stadium is being used for international matches has been solved by a simple but ingenious plan. They will be released above the stadium on chains like advertising blimps where they will promote local businesses and deter Godzilla attacks. This is the first initiative of its kind in the UK and Cardiff Council say:

"If all goes well and the death toll can be kept to a reasonable level then we see no reason why the scheme cannot be extended to include other existential threats like that big thing from Cloverfield or even giant robots piloted by tiny men pulling levers".

Jurassic Perk

The dinosaur compound which many say has spoilt the otherwise attractive scenic nature of the local environment.

Our on-the-spot reporter can officially bring you dramatic new developments in the ongoing saga of Kim Jong Un's proposed Godzilla nursery in the Swansea Bay Tidal Lagoon. Since we first revealed the plans to a stunned lower Swansea Valley and the surrounding districts, concerns have been raised within the local community. To address these concerns local businessmen Darren Coeliac and Vejay Polony of Coeliac and Polony Genetics (CPG) have built a dinosaur compound on the outskirts of the city ready to house a Giganotosaurus army should it become necessary

Planning permission was initially refused on the basis that there was already a proposal for an army of giant marauding hell beasts bent on the destruction of civilisation and a second such site would be an infringement of intellectual property. All such objections vanished however when CPG promised unlimited dinosaur rides for the children of councillors with a three-month introductory offer of replacement children should any unavoidable shreddings occur

Our undercover reporter gets slightly too close for comfort but will be fondly remembered by some people in the office. And it's not like it will even make secret Santa any cheaper because it doesn't work like that.

The dinosaur compound consists of twenty-foot-high adamantium and titanium mesh-based walls surrounded by an electrified fence which utilises the latest smart meter technology coupled with an automatic uSwitch app to keep the bills as low as possible. We asked CPG for an interview and they issued this statement via recently appointed head of publicity Sean Spicer.

The adamantium walls clearly visible behind the electric fence. What monsters lurk behind this imposing facade?

"Every step has been taken to reduce the risk of Giganotosaurus escape as anyone can see from the big walls and everything. We've got cameras and that so it's like on YouTube all the time so we're not going to get up to nothing and all that. So far almost none of our researchers have been consumed and definitely none from Swansea. Is Llanelli in Swansea? None from central Swansea. None from the centre of Swansea, you know the bit in the centre. Not fully consumed. Most people if you think about it can get by perfectly well with one foot.

In any event, I would like to reassure the public that we are fully insured and we compared all the insurances so we got the best one there is out there. It's really great insurance. It's fabulous insurance. What I think we can all agree on is the only effective answer to a bad guy with an army of viciously *psychotic, massively destructive rampaging lizard creatures is a good guy with an army of viciously psychotic, massively destructive rampaging lizard creatures.*

Let's make Swansea great again."

Well, that seems OK then I suppose.

Mothra in or out during Six Nations Tournament to be decided by toss of coin.

As the Six Nations Tournament is once again upon us, the question on everyone's lips this year is – 'giant mutant death dealing moth beasts; in or out?'

In years gone by the issue of whether the roof of the Principality Stadium would be open or closed was a major bone of contention. Traditionally, visiting teams have preferred it open due to the intensely oppressive atmosphere generated by the Welsh fans singing that song about the boy getting savaged by the family pet. This year the Trump administration backed Mothra breeding program means that up to ten Mothras could be in the Principality Stadium at the start of the game. Warren Gatland has expressed his preference for leaving them in during the game, arguing that 'they don't like the rain' and that 'several of them have season tickets'.

Chairman of the Board of Directors of the Welsh Rugby Union Gareth Davies insisted they should serve their agreed purpose as floating advertising hoardings, chained up like dinghies high above the stadium. *"We must maximise the commercial potential of these flamboyant but massively dangerous harbingers of death or we wouldn't be doing our duty to the fans or our commercial partners, many of whom own shares in the Mothra breeding program."*

The Scottish team have insisted the Mothras be let out for the duration of their game because Stuart Hogg has a thing about moths and if he hears them flapping it will do his head in and he won't come out of the dressing room. The Scottish coach also said that, due to their sustainability policy, their team costumes are all natural fibres which are like catnip to moths.

Rules state that the decision should be made on the toss of a coin, but Gareth Davies has said it should at least be best of three or even rock, paper, scissors. He dismissed claims that Scotland captain John Barclay was Dollar Academy rock, paper, scissors champion four years in a row between 2000 and 2004 as fake news.

Acting temporary substitute media relations executive Sean Spicer, formerly of the Ministry of Justice, formerly of Coeliac and Polony Genetics and formerly of The White House press corps had this to say.

"These are the best Mothra, they're really great Mothra. Everybody loves them all the time, they're so great. Roof open, roof closed, doesn't matter. They're the biggest Mothra, did you know that? Yeah. The biggest. They've got the wings. Those things coming out of their head. Everyone's going to love them, you'll see. You wait and see."

Swansea wants Nuclear Waste to feed Godzillas

Swansea Council's dreams of being home to a world-leading Tidal Lagoon have come a step closer after the Welsh Government launched a 12-week consultation to see if anywhere in Wales would volunteer to be the home of a nuclear waste disposal site. It would house the most radioactive material, some of which won't be safe for 250,000 years. The waste and its containers will occupy 650,000 cubic metres, which is about half the volume of the Principality Stadium.

Until now the future of the Lagoon had been uncertain. Regular Eye readers will recall that Kim Jong Un has promised financial backing for the project providing Swansea Council agrees to his plan of using it as a Godzilla nursery. Although one component of the Godzilla diet, laverbread, is readily available in Swansea another component, undiluted highly toxic nuclear waste has been more difficult to come by.

The prospect of hosting the so-called legacy waste above ground is not universally popular however and some critics have pointed out that the Port Tennant based self-storage facility 'Quality Containers' is not the requisite 1,000 metres below the surface. A spokesperson from Swansea Council issued a statement refuting the accusation that they have a cavalier attitude towards the safety of the public.

"As everyone knows Godzillas thrive on nuclear waste and they will need it close at hand for snacking purposes. There is also a great tradition of entertaining amongst the Godzilla community and if they have friends over how will it look if they can't put on a tidy spread? It would be embarrassing for them and I think you'll agree for the great City of Swansea if they had to burrow down a 1,000 metres every time they ran out of

canapés.

Swansea residents will be trained to recognise signs of radiation poisoning in their friends and relatives and hazmat suits will be issued to all toddlers irrespective of gender, racial origin, height, width even if they're ginger that can have one. This will be paid for by expected savings to the dental care budget as people's teeth fall out and no longer need to be filled.

In line with Swansea City Council's equal opportunities policy, this will be the most accessible nuclear waste dump in the world and will ensure the success of our great city at least until the Godzillas are big enough to rampage across Western Europe on a frenzied killing spree precipitating the fall of civilisation as we know it. So, you know, swings and roundabouts."

Mature Trees felled to form Swansea Godzilla Defences

Fifty mature trees have been cut down in Swansea City centre as work begins in earnest on the Godzilla defences in preparation for the inevitable senseless rampage which conservative estimates predict will annihilate 50% of all local businesses. An undisclosed number of people will also be killed and or mutilated. The move has not been without controversy as the defences will be mostly constructed using the trees from the city centre. When council workmen began felling the trees it sparked a storm of outrage across social media and aggrieved residents took to the streets.

Swansea Council's temporary, acting, interim, vice media liaison officer in charge of desperate last-ditch stands, Sean Spicer had this to say.

"These are the best trees, so beautiful. Beautiful mature trees. Imagine Godzilla, big Godzilla, with his tail. Breathing fire smashing stuff up. He's a big guy, the biggest and he's coming. Let's say he escapes; a lot of people escape. It happens all the time. Some people are escapologists, I love that word. Escapologist. It's a big word. One of the biggest.

Godzilla is not an escapologist, that requires years of training. Escapologists are fine, beautiful people, the best. But Godzilla is a ferocious, rampaging hell beast and we will have approximately 200 of them in the tidal lagoon at any given time so we have to assume some of them will escape. In that event and may the Lord our God protect us from such a calamity, praise be to Jesus, in that event, we will need to protect the city.

These once beautiful, amazing trees form part of our evil plan. Did I say evil plan? It's just a plan. The best plan, it's a great plan, beautiful plan. The plan is to use the trees as spiked barriers and that way we can corral the Godzillas into an area we have designated as the killing zone."

A woman in a hazmat outfit tugs Mr. Spicer by the arm and whispers in his ear.

The Dyfatty Senior Citizens Bowls Pavilion has undergone major changes recently, most notably the addition of nuclear armageddon strength electric fencing designed to hold escaped Godzillas for up to a period not exceeding a single human lunch-time.

"An area we have designated the fun time Godzilla play-zone. Some of you may have noticed the Dyfatty
Senior Citizens Bowls Pavilion has undergone some changes recently. We have installed high grade, the best. Beautiful, strong electric fencing. The escaped Godzillas will be pushed towards the Dyfatty Senior Citizens Bowls Pavilion using spikes made from the felled trees where they will be humanely..."

Mr. Spicer breaks off and leans towards the woman in the hazmat suit. They engage in a brief whispered discussion behind their hands. Mr. Spicer turns back to face the press.

"Annihilated in a humane way that is both fun and unexpected for the Godzilla hatchlings. This way we fully expect the human death toll to be kept below 2,500% for the equivalent non-Godzilla rampage designated time period, excluding persistent rain-related deaths. Any questions?"

Felling trees final stage in creation of marauding Orc army

Shocking scenes of destruction as Swansea Council feed local trees into the furnace of hell to forge an Orc army for one purpose. Two if you include guest editor spots on the Swansea Leader. Welsh Speaker essential.

Swansea City council is proud to announce the completion of Wales's first marauding Orc army. The signs have been there for all to see for the past year. The beastly ravaging of the built environment in the city centre, the seemingly pointless, never-ending, digging, digging, digging. Faceless workers in high-vis jackets, breaking their backs, hacking into the very foundations of the transport infrastructure. Exposing the dark, satanic bowels of The Kingsway, The Westway, Orchard Street, St Helens Road and anywhere else their festering industry wills them onto.

Swansea council, learning from the mistakes of Sauron the Necromancer, have put health and safety at the top of their agenda when creating a pitiless, psychopathic all-engulfing hoard of death-dealing maniacs. Note the use of actual red tape to symbolise the administrative nightmare of creating an unstoppable Orc army. #CityOfCulture

Acres of desolate scarring have turned the city centre into a Mordor like landscape of confusion with bewildered citizens desperately yearning for a simpler time. Having dug down to find the correct combination of stone and slime on which to work the sorcery of Morgoth the council has finally embarked on the ultimate stage of the enterprise. The felling of mature trees in the city centre will provide the fuel for the furnaces wherein the stone/slime-clay will be baked to a powerful substance harder than stone and more offensive than slime. From this substance will be crafted the mighty Orc army and the land shall tremble, probably.

The cover story about trees having '*caused damage to pavements, making them potential trip hazards*' was necessary to prevent Lampeter from getting the drop on Swansea. Lampeter council have been working on an Orc army since Christmas but are still in the evil plan stage. By fiercely protecting their intellectual property Swansea council have managed to manufacture an army of marauding soulless, killing machines well under budget and ahead of schedule.

Here we see the relentless slaughter of the local flora for the entirely sensible reason of providing an expendable bulwark against the much anticipated Godzilla Armageddon.

Now the work is complete Swansea will have full protection against the Godzilla army set to descend upon Wales's second city with the completion of the tidal lagoon power station. Up until now, they have relied on a makeshift system involving Dyfatty Bowling green and some wooden spikes.

After an Orc raiding party disemboweled fifteen Japanese

tourists at Oystermouth castle sparking an international incident, Swansea Council's temporary, acting, interim, vice media liaison officer in charge of plausible deniability, Sean Spicer had this to say.

"There was good and bad on both sides. The Orc is well known for its traditional values. We don't know the full story here. We don't know if all the Japanese had the correct paperwork. A lot of them were taking photographs, something which Orcs find very offensive, they should have known that. Who knows whose fault it was? We may never find out. I think there needs to be an investigation into exactly what the Japanese tourists were doing there, what they were up to at lunchtime in a public place. Taking photographs. Did they have a permit? I'm not saying we should launch a counter-strike at this stage. I think everyone needs to calm down. Any questions?"

Tidal Lagoon saved by North Korean Denuclearization

Now that Kim Jong Un and Donald Trump are BFFs, it appears the Swansea Bay Tidal Lagoon project has received a massive boost. As regular readers will know, the North Korean despot has been funding the development of the tidal lagoon in order to rear an army of Godzillas with which to threaten Western civilization. His vow to denuclearize means Mr. Kim will now be more reliant than ever on the destructive capabilities being hatched in South Wales. In order to ensure the denuclearization of the Korean Peninsula is carried out as promised, Mr. Trump has made an unprecedented gesture of goodwill.

He has secured the services of Liberace and Tim Curry to entertain punters in the underwater caravan park which will be an integral feature of the Lagoon when it opens in the future. Mr. Ace will play all his greatest hits and will accompany Mr. Curry as he recreates some of the more family-friendly scenes from The Rocky Horror Picture Show. Swansea council will be installing anti trample cages above the caravans to prevent them being obliterated by the Godzillas as they wander around the lagoon searching for signs of civilization to wreak havoc upon. The cages are thought to be based on the safety barriers currently being used throughout the city to stop pedestrians stumbling into the gaping maw of hell from which the marauding Orc army will emerge should the Godzillas ever threaten central Swansea.

These cages are currently being used by Swansea council to protect its citizens from thousands of slavering maniacs forged in the depths of hell. 80% discount on business rates due to charitable status of Orc army.

The underwater caravan park is to be the biggest in Europe. The only one larger in the world is New Atlantis, part of The Walt Disney World Resort in Florida. New Atlantis covers the entire bed of Lake Apopka and has all the facilities of onshore hotels including many of the familiar Disney Park characters. For reasons of authenticity, the characters are not allowed to wear breathing apparatus, so they mostly just float around on top of the water bumping into boats and shouting for help.

The exception to this rule is Donald Duck, whose tail invariably fills up with water and drags him straight to the bottom where he is able to access the coin-operated emergency oxygen pipes located every 300 metres.

Swansea's Tidal Lagoon underwater caravan park will also feature colourful costume characters. They will hang out in and around CKs supermarket on the central concourse and visitors will be able to approach them to receive complimentary cans of Special Brew and scratch cards. Reveal three faces of Kim Jong Un to win the freedom of Pyongyang and a Godzilla proof ankle bracelet. #CityOfCulture

Orcs destroy world's first tidal power lagoon dream

Plans to build the world's first tidal power lagoon have been thrown out by the UK government. The shock decision was inevitable as soon as the main backer Kim Jong Un pulled all funding after twenty thousand Orcs descended on the Crymlyn Burrows Amazon fulfilment centre and killed all the Godzillas in the breeding program. The Godzillas had reached stage three maturity and were almost ready to be transferred to the Tidal Lagoon.

Two of them had been helping out in the returns department on weekends and another three had taken Fulfilment Associate positions although one is on long-term sick complaining of stress. Barry, known in the fulfilment centre as 'the cheeky Godzilla' has been employee of the month three times and was in charge of a team in Fulfilment Loss Prevention. Another fifteen have been unable to obtain work visas so normally just play football in the canteen.

The marauding Orc army was bred by Swansea City council for one purpose. To destroy the Godzillas, should they ever threaten the people of Swansea. Unfortunately, Tricia Jones from Killay got into an argument with Barry one day when she said he was looking at her funny. She took the matter up with her line manager who called Barry in for an HR interview. Just an informal chat. Barry panicked and accidentally reduced the IT support department to rubble. Tricia messaged the Orcs on FaceBook who immediately launched an all-out attack.

Scenes of carnage and more carnage greeted employees as they tried to enter work the following day only to be greeted by the members of an Orc army, one of whom was carrying a gigantic bomb as he ran across the Aneurin Bevan car park. The resulting explosion ripped a massive hole in the side of the building and the Orcs swarmed through, looking for the Godzillas.

A battle royal ensued with the Godzillas initially gaining the upper hand. At one point it looked as if Amazon would come to the rescue. Jeff Bezos, taking advantage of his Amazon Prime membership, personally ordered fifteen thousand killer drones and sent them to kill the Orcs. However, the Orcs were not at home at the time so the drones executed their neighbours instead. Day and night the battle raged but the Orcs eventually did what they were designed to do and the last Godzilla fell before their brutal onslaught at 10:15 am earth time.

Swansea Council's temporary, acting, interim, vice media liaison officer in charge of Game of Thrones Style Plot Twists, Sean Spicer had this to say.

"The Godzillas were humble, beautiful creatures. We wish them all the best with being dead and that. I met a guy on the way here and you know what he said to me? He said to me, 'The Godzillas are great and everything but I wish we had something like a marauding Orc army to maybe kill them all if they step out of line'. You know he said that to me? And I thought, gee... And so I think we've all learned something today. Any questions?"

Corbyn creates Doddzilla to save Tidal Lagoon

Jeremy Corbyn (destroyer of worlds) has opened a back channel to formerly despotic tyrant Kim Jong Un in order to secure the future of Swansea's tidal lagoon/Godzilla nursery. Mr. Corbyn has also reached out to the famously anti-Tory city of Liverpool by announcing the creation of Doddzilla. This hybrid of funny man Ken Dodd and the infamous Godzilla is the creation of Neath-based mad scientists and will dwell within the Swansea Bay Tidal Lagoon.

Regular readers will remember Kim Jong Un's Godzilas, originally destined for the lagoon, were destroyed by a marauding Orc army in a close-run contest of brawn Vs brawn. This led to massive unemployment issues within the Orc community who were bred for a single purpose. Having achieved this purpose their limited skill set meant they struggled to find alternative occupations. The soft skills, increasingly important in today's diverse jobs market were totally lacking and they found it impossible to comply with even the most basic health and safety instructions.

The relaunch of the tidal lagoon project to breed the Ken Dodd, Godzilla hybrid for the North Korean dictator will bring a much-needed jobs boost to Swansea and the marauding Orc army in particular. Mr. Corbyn has sworn to see the tidal lagoon project resurrected as part of his green jobs revolution. However, the prospect of Ken Dodd rampaging across South Wales, destroying whole communities with dragon breath whilst simultaneously cheering them up has angered many.

Mrs. Daphne Flangepocket of Ystradgynlais wanted none of it. *"What about the children? How are they supposed to grow up if a tormented genetic freak tramples them into the ground and incinerates the twisted remains? It's the thin end of the wedge."*

A spokesman for the Orc army Boragg Khazgroz called for calm. *"We will destroy the living and the dead with equal relish. Our armies will lay waste to the Doddzilla menace. Any who dare stand between us and our sworn mission shall feel the wrath of the thousand, thousand beasts at our command. Darkness and pain is the destiny of all our enemies for we have one purpose."*

He has since been dismissed from the Spontex 2019 Human Resources Graduate Program after it was discovered he lied on his CV.

The Trump/Liberace Dichotomy

After seeing the famous photograph of Nigel Farage and Donald Trump in Trump's gold lift in Trump towers it struck me how much like Liberace's his taste in interior décor was. I got a little bit obsessed with the idea that Trump was in fact Liberace and that the gold lift was his toilet so when you see Liberace mentioned in these articles just think Trump. And imagine him in a toilet with Nigel Farage and they've both got their thumbs up. Similarly, when you see Trump mentioned, just picture the coiffured figure of Liberace relaxing in the opulence of his Rococo boudoir, smelling of Chanel.

Donald Trump radicalised after visit to Cardiff Hotel

Tudor Grehamby of Llanpumsaint told yesterday of his seminal role in radicalising Donald Trump. Tudor, along with his wife Glendolynne, runs the holistic therapy institute for mindfulness as part of the sustainably integrated complementary centre for the politically spiteful just outside Llanpumsaint off the B4301.

He and his wife radicalised the Trumps in 2015 when Donald and Melania were on an all-inclusive at the Radisson Blu in Cardiff. Tired of the glitz and glamour of the capital they spotted Tudor's leaflet in the hotel welcome pack and were initially drawn to the Therapeutic Nasal Coma Induction and the complimentary Ear Candles.

As the premier member of the South West Wales association of alternative health and lifestyle gurus the centre offers, amongst other therapies:

- Crystal healing
- Therapeutic Horseback Riding
- Rebirthing (breathing)
- Reiki
- Enemas
- Rolfing (Structural Integration)
- Yoga
- Extreme Radicalisation Therapy

Because organisations like ISIS, the Ku Klux Klan (KKK) and the World Wrestling Federation (WWF) are putting so much effort into their social media presence nowadays they suddenly find they don't have the resources for face-to-face radicalisation anymore. Outsourcing the work using franchise models based on local licenses, bespoke training and luncheon vouchers has seen their reach broaden and cash flow improve dramatically. For cash-strapped alternative therapy centres, it has been a Godsend and West Wales has been quick to take up the slack.

Interviewed earlier this year Tudor was very proud of his part in developing Donald Trump's political outlook.

"Well when he come to us, he'd never even heard of politics, he could barely make a sandwich. He'd seen one of our leaflets in the hotel and to be honest he just fancied a bit of therapeutic horseback riding and maybe an enema or two. Now I was on it like a shot because we got a three for two deal Fridays and Tuesdays and we get the commission on the extreme radicalisation therapy as part of the franchise.

We offer radical Islam, radical Christianity, radical yoga and extreme right-wing ideology with an upgrade to Make insert name here Great Again for an additional £2.50, lunch included. As a businessman, he's got an eye for a bargain and he went for the extreme right-wing package. Melania was a bit more reserved so she skipped lunch.

Well imagine my surprise when we saw him on the TV and he do be running for the president of the United States of America. Fair play to him, he'd remembered everything and his hair looked lovely."

Since the election of Donald Trump, Tudor has been to the White House 15 times and on one occasion was required to send out for a horse and three additional super plus enema pumps.

Trump's emotional Support Wig enters Rehab in Wales

Donald Trump's emotional support wig has been flown to Wales to enter rehab for a substance abuse problem. The wig, made entirely from an illegal Mexican fighting Guinea Pig is staying at the palatial Woofers Paradise just West of Swansea in a move designed to bring order to the Western world. The Wig has a checkered history and first made its name in the seedy underworld activity of Mexican Guinea Pig wrestling going by the name of El Conejillo De Indias Big Ginger. Masked Guinea Pigs regularly wrestle for money in tavernas and underground car parks but little is known about the activity because of the first rule of Guinea Pig wrestling.

The wig, which was a Guinea Pig at the time, was notorious for its vicious temper and impetuous behaviour. It had been banned from most of the wrestling tournaments partly because of its underhand methods and partly because of its habit of turning up without its kit and no note. Eventually, it was killed by the Guadalahara mob for refusing to take a dive and that's when it was acquired on the black market by Melania Trump. She was looking for a replacement for Donald's previous wig, which he had been wearing since 1982 and which became eligible for early retirement.

At first, the wig was a big talking point. Nestling snugly with his existing red thatch it was quite a hit at dinner parties and costume balls but as the months past it became noticeably unpredictable and on the 5th of June 2013, it became sentient.

Theories vary about how this could happen. Some say the wig is possessed by the ghost of El Conejillo De Indias Big Ginger, some say it was subject to a massive overdose of Gamma radiation. Others have alleged Russian meddling. Nobody knows for sure but one thing is certain, from that day forward, its powerful consciousness controlled everything Donald Trump said and did. All went well for a while and many credit the wig with Trump's victory in the 2016 presidential elections. The rot began to set in however, the day after the inauguration.

The wig became enraged by the low turnout and started drinking in private. Day by day it whispered more and more insane things into Trump's ear.

'Tell footballers they need to stand up'.

'Say Kim Jong Un has a rubbish nuclear button'.

'Share that Britain First video, they seem like nice people'.

Over and over again it told him to do more and more outrageous things until a sharp-eyed secret service agent realised what was happening. The next day the secret service, white house staff, defence staff and several of the cleaners staged an intervention where they told the wig how its actions had affected them and how they had heard of a very good facility on the A48 just past the Pont Abraham service station. Reluctantly, the wig relinquished the levers of power and was escorted from the building.

If all goes well the wig should be able to resume duties within the month, meanwhile it has been replaced by a sedated chinchilla and a Photoshop technician.

Nigel Farage and Liberace share caravan in Fishguard

Wales is doubly blessed this summer by the presence of two major celebrities. Nigel Farage has been invited to spend two weeks in Liberace's static caravan in Fishguard Holiday Park and he's jumped at the chance. Sick of slumming it in Brussels and determined to show off the benefits of a good old British staycation Mr. Farage packed his bags and set his Sat Nav to fun.

From the bathroom of Liberace's multi-million-pound mobile home Mr. Farage chatted with reporters and handed out tea and cough sweets.

Liberace (real name Gareth Onllwyn Glynog Christmas Ap Gareth) can trace his family tree back as far as the 11th Century when an ancestor 'Gareth Yr Chwaraewr' travelled the country telling tales from the Mabinogion and playing requests on a rudimentary piano. A bad case of Carpal Tunnel Syndrome put paid to his vagabond lifestyle and he settled down in Fishguard eventually rising to middle management in the environmental health department. In 1085 he was awarded the status of Rat-finder General a title the family still carries to this day.

To celebrate his rich heritage Liberace invested in an 11.2 metre Victory Capri static caravan with a built in DVD player and microwave. Once a year he journeys from Las Vegas to Fishguard to spend two weeks with his feet up but last year he caused a stir when his controversial loft conversion blocked the views of Goodwick for Gwen and Hilary Davis-Hughes.

At the time, Gwen expressed her disappointment to reporters and pretty much anyone else after she'd had a few pints.

"We're only here two weeks a year and that fat slag comes

and shoves a fucking dormer on his roof. Can't see nothing out the front except that twat in his underpants banging out Somewhere Over the Fucking Rainbow *on a Steinway and cramming Pringles into his tear stained face. He should be working his issues out with a shrink, not six bottles of Lambrini and a carbs binge. He's dragged the whole area right down. Her indoors has been on at me since we got here. What am I supposed to do? If he keeps this up, I'm going to get round there and fucking twat him".*

A substantial financial settlement resolved the issue but the bad blood persists and both Mr Farage and Liberace have been getting what they describe as 'Funny looks' from Gwen and Hilary all week. Undaunted the two friends set out on a cliff walk this morning, determined to make the best of the weather and to:

'get away from the hurly burly of our celebrity lifestyles and just live like normal, common *people for a few hours'.*

We wish them all the best and can confirm that this is exactly the sort of behaviour that is going to Make Britain Great Again, only more so. Self-guided tours of Liberace's static caravan are available from Fishguard Holiday Park between September and June. Visitors are advised to leave some money in the honesty box and to replace the key under the doormat when they leave.

Shock as Cardiff loses Dr Who to Fishguard in a bid to #MakeDrWhoGreatAgain

In a shock decision, the BBC has cast Liberace as the new Dr Who. A perfect storm of nostalgia for the good old days of yore (when everything was great) and government-imposed austerity has forced the BBC to bring back the rocking sets and floppy fingered monsters we all knew and loved. Filming will be relocated from Cardiff Bay to Fishguard Holiday Park to accommodate Liberace's busy schedule and interior scenes of the TARDIS are to be shot in the luxurious en-suite toilet of his 11.2 metre Victory Capri static caravan.

Other cutbacks mean there will be no external locations but fans of the good old days of yore (when everything was great) have a special treat coming their way. Nigel Farage has been signed up as the Dr's new assistant and looks set to play the son of Danny Pink. Whovians will remember Danny, love interest of Clara Oswald, played by Samuel Anderson first appearing in series 8. Mr. Farage spoke to our reporter just after the news broke and had these words to say.

"I'm glad to be doing my bit to Make Dr Who Great Again. I think the public is getting pretty sick of all this intergalactic travel and want to see good, honest, British stories. Liberace's got one of the best toilets in the world and we should be showing it to the world. I remember when the villains in Dr Who couldn't turn a knob without their fingers bending back.

That's what the public want. I've already started glueing false nails onto a pair of green Marigold Gloves ready for the close-ups. I'm sick of people whingeing about how it's going to look rubbish and cheap and nasty and dated and embarrassing and unintentionally funny and... It's done now; they should all get behind it. Beer and fags are great, aren't they?"

A spokesman for the BBC said: *"Nigel will be Nigel."*

Fishguard Holiday Park resident Gwen Davis-Hughes had this to say.

"It's bad enough he's playing his piano day and night but if that Fat Slag thinks he's going to have the BBC tramping all over my Mind-your-own-business he can stick it where the sun don't shine. Me and Hilary likes to have our bondage sessions twice a week rain or shine and she can belt it out even through the ball-gag. Sounds like a crop duster taxiing for takeoff some days. Fair play to her, she's enthusiastic. If they starts calling for quiet on the set I'm going to be straight round there with a riding crop and five kilos of nipple clamps. This is a residential area. I'm not having it."

A representative of the Fishguard Holiday Park said: *"Gwen will be Gwen"*.

Swansea Market controversial Stained Glass Window

International pianist and legendary Cymrophile Liberace created a stir this week by offering Swansea City a magnificent Stained-Glass window for its indoor market. The sequined soloist committed to spend £5 million to replace the newly renewed windows and transform the showpiece retail environment into a world-class tourist attraction. Inspired by Swansea's part in last year's successful Brexit referendum the coiffured concerto crooner decided to dedicate a work of art to its chief architect Nigel Farage.

Liberace has taken an unnaturally keen interest in Brexit since forming a close friendship with ex UKIP leader Nigel Farage. The unlikely duo first met when Liberace signed up for a training day organised by Mr. Farage as part of the latter's attempt to establish a sustainable, organic horse meat shop on the Balls Pond Road. The training covered basic cutting techniques, soil association national standards of good practice and personality disorders in foreign horses.

Seduced by Mr Farage's 'magnetic personality' and cut-price horse meat, Liberace established a tax refuge in Fishguard and has fallen in love with his adopted country. He was delighted when Swansea voted decisively for Brexit in the 2017 referendum and vowed to commemorate the event. The window, set to be 'bigger than anything in Europe' is planned for the North facing side of the market. Sources confirm the subject matter will be a 'tasteful reproduction' of the historic first meeting between the two men which, for undisclosed reasons, took place in the toilet of the Liberace's static caravan in Fishguard.

The window, at its summit, will be over 60 feet tall and will stretch the entire length of the market, bathing shoppers in the golden glow of Brexit for all eternity. Market stall holder, Glyndwr McGonagall-Khan, had this to say.

"It'll make the cheese look funny, you can't deny it."

Sean Spicer, temporary acting project vice spokesman in charge of image maintenance and cheese related issues said:

"This is going to be the best window. The biggest... Bigger than anything in Europe and better colours too. We've got all the best colours. Gold, yellow, red, all the colours. It's going to make the cheese look great. Sausages too. It's going to bring jobs to Swansea. Not like that dinosaur farm or that nuclear waste dump in Port Tennant."

Swansea council have welcomed the news of a jobs boost and in a gesture of support have decided to reconfigure the city centre road layout. The gesture will serve no practical purpose but it will give residents a sense of continuity during the construction process.

Make Wales Great Again
#MWGAMWGAMWGA

Due to the massively successful Brexit referendum it is strongly anticipated that Britain will definitely be great again in the very near future. As a result of this momentous event First Minister, the Rt Hon Carwyn Jones AM, has decided unilaterally to abandon the system of advertising the Terrorism Threat Level (TTL) and replace it in Wales with more useful Level of Greatness (LoG). Please see below our handy guide to the new system which will come into force immediately. We thank you for your compliance and appreciate your alertness in all matters of greatness.

What the levels of greatness mean

LoG are designed to give a broad indication of the likelihood of greatness.

QUITE GOOD. Wales still mainly known as an international unit of deforestation

RATHER GOOD. Wales has a musical legend under the age of seventy, who's not in prison.

GREAT. Wales beats New Zealand at rugby without the use of knives, guns or nipple tweaking.

FULL ON GREAT. Someone from Wales gets to be boss of something really important in England, maybe even Prime Minister

BLOODY FANTASTIC. A successful invasion of Patagonia and Wrexham AFC in the Premier League.

How are greatness levels decided?

The Greatness Level for Wales (GLW) is set by the Department of Actual Greatness (DAG).

Welsh Government is responsible for setting the greatness levels based on sporting, musical and other domestic and international accomplishments.

In reaching a judgement on the appropriate greatness level in any given circumstance several factors need to be taken into account.

These include:

Available intelligence. It is rare that specific accomplishment information is available and can be relied upon. More often, judgments about Welsh greatness will be based on a wide range of information, which is often fragmentary, including the level and nature of current sporting/cultural/economic activity, comparison with greatness levels in other countries and previous spontaneous outbreaks of greatness. Intelligence is only ever likely to reveal part of the picture.

Greatness capability. An examination of what is known about the capabilities of the Welsh Rugby Union and the method they may use based on previous encounters with The All Blacks or from intelligence. This would also analyse the potential scale of the any victory over The All Blacks.

Greatness intentions. Using intelligence and publicly available information to examine the overall aims of sports or music stars and the ways they may achieve them including what sort of products they would consider endorsing. A German car or a posh perfume would indicate intentions of greatness.

Timescale. The greatness level expresses the likelihood of achievements in the near term. We know from past incidents that some achievements take years to plan, while others are put together more quickly. In the absence of specific intelligence, a judgement will need to be made about how close greatness might be to fruition. Greatness levels do not have any set expiry date but are regularly subject to review in order to ensure that they remain current.

How should you respond?

Greatness levels in themselves do not require specific responses from the public. They are a tool for government officials working across different sectors of the Central Unified Notification Team (C Team) and the DAG to use in determining what Boasting Standard (BS) response may be required.

Vigilance is vital regardless of the current national level of greatness. It is especially important given the expected increase in national greatness. Sharing national greatness levels with the general public keeps everyone informed. It explains the context for the various government measures (for example smug, self-important announcements or press conferences about roads) which we may encounter in our daily lives.

If you have information about possible greatness, call the Greatness Hotline: 02016 666 666.

The Greatness Hotline is for tip-offs and confidential information. For warnings about anti greatness activity or other urgent threats please call 999.

Wales to be Ground Zero for Making Stuff Great Again #MWGA

A furious Twitter row has erupted between Kim Jong-un and Donald Trump over which one of them is going to Make Wales Great Again. Kim Jong-un's now infamous plan for a Godzilla nursery in the Swansea Bay tidal lagoon was disparaged by Trump in a series of tweets this week. The tweets claimed the US-backed Mothra breeding program in the Millennium Stadium would Make Wales Great Again. The leader of the Democratic People's Republic of Korea retaliated by saying his legion of Godzillas would put Wales on the map and make it 'feared and respected the world over'.

Mr. Trump has taken Wales to his heart since spending a *'lovely weekend'* being radicalised in Llanpumsaint. *"Wales has the best radicalisers. Those guys... Let me tell you... When they get radicalising... They're really going to Make Wales Great Again. So good... Nice lunch. Four stars"*

Mr. Kim has vowed to work with First Minister the Rt Hon Carwyn Jones AM *'to advance under the leadership of the party and with strong faith in sure victory.'* He went on to say *"The Godzilla army should always maintain a highly agitated state and be equipped with full fighting readiness so as to smash the enemies with a single stroke."*

Mr. Jones reiterated his commitment to the future development of Wales.

"The Welsh Labour government is very proud of our record of securing inward investment. Both the Godzilla nursery and the Mothra breeding program are signs of a healthy Welsh economy that is open for business. I understand there have been some disagreements between The US and North Korea and both

have threatened the total annihilation of great swathes of the M4 corridor but in England, under a conservative government you have to pay to park when you visit a hospital."

The hashtag #MWGA has been trending since last Thursday as a result of both Mr. Trump and Mr. Kim making it a personal crusade to ensure Wales has all the benefits normally associated with being the battleground for nuclear mutated giant death dealing city destroyers. New York and Tokyo were sleepy backwater towns before being threatened by King Kong and Godzilla respectively. Both rose to world prominence as a direct result of being attacked by freakishly large and inexplicably angry creatures from the Pacific Ocean.

If Wales is to become great again we will all have to get behind these ambitious plans for widespread carnage. This is our chance to once again be the proud nation that led the industrial revolution; to hold our heads up and announce our presence on the world stage. Let battle commence.

Welsh Government upping the game with conspiracies consultation #MWGA

The Conspiracies Committee was set up in 1999 as a matter of urgency by the then First Secretary Alun Michael to examine the possibility of covering up government activity in devolved areas where it was deemed the public would either not grasp the complexity of national security issues or would object to public money being spent on the practice of feeding thousands of Welsh citizens to rapacious inter-galactic time travelling Nazis in a craven act of appeasement designed to secure ministers a seat on the mothership after the inevitable destruction of mankind.

The Conspiracies Committee has met every second Tuesday of every month ever since but has yet to get to grips with the intractable paperwork involved with mounting a conspiracy in a modern democracy. Because of this, no conspiracies have been discussed in 18 years and Wales now runs the risk of being the only nation in wider Europe with no secretive plans to place the capricious whims of a moneyed elite above the rights of the wider population. To date, the WG has relied on incompetence and or pointless in fighting to achieve this. A state of affairs which any right-thinking person knows cannot carry on if we are to hold our heads up on the world stage.

This consultation outlines the Welsh government's proposed conspiracies which, if implemented, would catapult us into the top tier of international bogeymen for the tin foil hat brigade and that guy you went to school with who is now big on twitter and occasionally tries to get you to sign a petition against pig farming on Mars.

The proposed conspiracies would lead to a streamlining of clandestine operations within Wales and speed up the development of activities including but not exclusively:

- Secret Handshakes.
- Alien abduction denial scenarios.
- Vast underground complexes housing alien and inter-dimensional technology.
- Satanic ritual etiquette training.
- Crop circle compensation schemes.
- The creation of the post of Conspiracies Commissioner.
- What conspiracies are proposed?
- Random alien abductions.

Official figures show that although sightings of UFOs in Wales far exceed the national average, the number of abductions is far below what would be expected from a nation of three million people. With this in mind, it is proposed that a target of no fewer than 10 abductions a year be set for the first 10 years. It is also proposed to instigate a designated program of crop circle development featuring the faces of local celebrities.

Satanic Ritual etiquette training.

It has long been a bone of contention that when WG ministers attend international events they are ill-equipped for even the most rudimentary satanic shenanigans. Vaughan Gething *(The WG Cabinet Secretary for Health)* was humiliated at a Bilderberg Group away day last year when he didn't even know which trouser leg to roll up and had to cover up the awkward silence with a Craig Charles impersonation which bordered on racism.

Vast underground complexes housing alien and inter-dimensional technology

In fairness, this one already exists but this proposal would mean the Welsh government would be given a set of keys.

Crop circle compensation schemes

See alien abductions.

Secret handshakes

This would be decided by a simple yes-no referendum.

The creation of the post of Conspiracies Commissioner

If conspiracies lack satisfactory levels of evil, secrecy or a fully costed Welsh language scheme the public must have a means of redress. The Conspiracies Commissioner will have the power to summon witnesses and if necessary, suspend all conspiracy activity for a period not exceeding the lifetime of the human race.

Consultation Questions

- The Welsh Government is seeking views on the proposed conspiracies and their practical application. In particular:
- Do you agree with the proposed conspiracies?
- Do you have any further comments in relation to the proposed conspiracies?
- Have you considered the extent to which the implementation of random alien abductions will impact on local authorities in Wales?

Next Steps

Following the close of the consultation, all responses will be analysed and any necessary amendments made to the draft conspiracies. A summary of consultation responses will also be published on the Welsh Government website. It is intended that the draft conspiracies will be laid before the National Assembly for Wales so that they can come into effect on or before 31 March 2019.

Conspiracies feedback leaves government wondering if the public are up to something

The conspiracies consultation we reported on three weeks ago has had a mixed reception amongst the Welsh public. Some have reacted positively, enthusing about the ambitious nature of the satanic ritual etiquette training in particular.

Unfortunately, not all feedback has been so positive. The development of a Welsh conspiracy, in particular, has drawn criticism from consumer groups and tin foil hat manufacturers alike. Consumer groups have called into question the need for a specifically Welsh government conspiracy when there are perfectly good UK wide conspiracies. They see it as nothing more than tokenism and an unnecessary duplication of efforts. Tin foil hat manufacturers have stated the need for eternal vigilance.

Grant Bestman-Chapstick of the Welsh consumer rights group MyCym said

"This is typical of the sort of short-sighted parochialism we've come to expect from this government. They've got proper conspiracies going on in Westminster with giant lizards and the royal family and gerbils and stuff. It's been going on since the Knights Templar and that, everyone knows it. It's not the best use of government resources. The Welsh language translation bill alone is going to be ruinous. We'll be using twice as much invisible ink for all the secret messages. And where are the clandestine meetings going to be? Some posh hotel in mid-Wales no doubt. This money could be better spent on nice new kidneys for people or a big boat."

Mary Min of the tin foil hat manufacturers association of Wales alleged there were darker motives. *"This whole conspiracy consultation is just some sort of conspiracy if you ask me."*

Devenauld Fitzpatrick of The Conspiracies Committee which meets monthly wanted to assure the public its money was being well spent.

"The need for a specifically Welsh conspiracy has been self evident ever since the National Assembly for Wales was established. If we are to keep pace with the world of social media, then we need to be considered a danger to people's freedom in a way that's relevant to them. In a way they can relate to and become outraged by at their own convenience. I was even considering a fake conspiracy just for an added layer of deviousness. But because of the Welsh language translation budget and the risk assessment and ecological impact assessment and the UNCRC impact assessment and requisitioning the paperclips there was no real financial advantage in not having a real one so that's why we decided to throw it open to public consultation.

Now they all think we're up to something. Which makes me think they're up to something."

George Soros Conspiracy, Conspiracy

Evidence is emerging that Billionaire philanthropist George Soros has been made up by 'The Deep State' mostly to make millionaire philanthropists feel inadequate. Sources as reputable as Alex Jones (of The One Show) have been saying for years that Soros is a fictional character much like Australia and British Prime Minister Theresa May. Many readers will recall, it was discovered last month, that Theresa May is currently being played by an out of work Shakespearean actor-manager, 'Driftwood Thoringer IV'.

Useful Idiots

Jones has repeatedly called on the mainstream media to prove the existence of Soros who she describes as 'the greatest trick played on humanity since Christopher Columbus convinced everyone the world was round'. She claims people who say they have met Soros are 'all actors and computer-generated personas, part of the plot to trick the world.' In an interview with her namesake on Infowars Jones asserted that it was all a fiction spread by the useful idiots on the left for some reason or other and she challenged viewers to prove they had met the real George Soros.

The truth is over by there.

Conspiracy Theory

So far so whack-job conspiracy theory I hear you say but I did some real investigative journalism myself and discovered that none of my Facebook friends had ever met him. Even more convincingly, none of their friends had met him either. For someone so much in the public eye, that seemed really strange. But what finally made alarm bells start to ring was when I discovered that the name George Soros has eleven letters

In Numerology the number 11 is a master number and represents inspiration, illumination, and spiritual enlightenment. 11 is the Gateway or Portal: the doorway between two worlds – between the 3rd dimensional and the 5th-dimensional worlds. This means that a person called George Soros would not be able to travel to the fourth dimension. Of course, this is where the lizard creatures running the organisation that controls Deep Government originate. Also, the word illumination sounds a bit like Illuminati so you know…

Rhosllanerchrugog

Each of these things on their own might sound innocent enough but put them all together and they make a compelling case. The man accused of having a controlling interest in almost every high-level conspiracy of the last thirty years turns out to be a fictional character created by a low to mid-level conspiracy. If we have learned anything from this sordid episode it's that the world is definitely flat and the Moon is from Rhosllanerchrugog but it was so difficult to pronounce the ancients decided to say it was up in the sky.

Prison Loans

In an announcement sneaked out under cover of Boris Johnson's groundbreaking idea of a cross-channel bridge, Minister for Justice The Rt Hon David Gauke MP, set out his plans for 'Prison Loans'. The idea is, prisoners should pay for the cost of their imprisonment but that 'prisoner loans' would be made available to those who could not afford to do so.

A statement from the National Committee of Inquiry into Prison Conditions, reads:

"We do not underestimate the strength of feeling on the issue of seeking a contribution towards rehabilitation costs. A detailed assessment of the issues has, however, convinced us that the arguments in favour of a contribution to rehabilitation costs from prisoners in 'work' are strong, if not widely appreciated.

They relate to equity between social groups, broadening imprisonment opportunities, equity with 'part-time' prisoners who are electronically tagged or on suspended sentences, strengthening the prisoner role in rehabilitation, and identifying a new source of income that can be ring-fenced for proper wrongguns."

Mr. Gauke made it clear.

"I have sound research that shows prisoners would appreciate their rehabilitation more if they paid for it. A lot of prisoners, let's be honest, go in there because it's paid for and they have a great time. I know a lot of people who went to prison because they didn't want to go to work and they probably came out with a bit of a rubbish CV and as a taxpayer, I resent that and I know the man on the Clapham Omnibus certainly does".

Temporary project spokesman Sean Spicer on loan from Coeliac and Polony Genetics had this to say. *"Prisoners will not be expected to pay back the loans until they 'earn' more than £20K a year. The money will be used to build the best prisons. Bars, doors, everything... Food... Dogs, everything... Those things on the doors, the swingey things that they look through in the films but with glass on so they can't get stabbed in the eye with a sharpened toothbrush or something.*

Obviously, there will be penalties for not paying back the loans, maybe a fine or imprisonment. We might have to work on that one; perhaps we can just get someone to punch them. A lot of people don't like it when you rub polystyrene together so it squeaks. We could do that to them. Anyway, this is a terrific policy, it's the best policy and the public love it. Everyone should do it. Has anybody got a fag, I'm gasping?"

The Swansea Road Works

I only intended to write one article about Swansea Roadworks because, well how many articles can you write about essentially nothing happening for a very long time. As it turns out, quite a few. The roadworks quickly proved to be my most popular subject and I realised I'd struck a nerve, not just in Swansea but everywhere seemingly endless and pointless roadworks inconvenience both drivers and pedestrians alike.

Armed with a camera and faced by a rapidly changing yet consistently chaotic city scape, I found the stories just flowed. Every time I think I've finally said all there is to say on the subject, something even more bizarre happens to drag me back in. As I write this there is no end in sight and I'm just petty enough to hope it never changes.

Will we ever know why we are here?

Before the big bang, there was nothing. No time and no space. The big bang had nowhere to go so its expansion created space, as it was pushed out by unfathomable energy and the simple fact of change within its structure created time. It was small now it is big.

Fundamental particles obeying the laws of physics coalesced into atoms of hydrogen and helium. Eventually, after billions of years, these atoms began to form stars and these stars lived and died and out of their death throws were forged all the elemental particles we find today.

Unimaginable pressures within dying stars produced gold, diamonds, uranium and iron. After billions more years these heavy elements formed planets which circled their stars and crashed and burned or withered and blinked out of existence.

At long last, our own solar system was born and within it, Earth. A water world gifted with all the elements necessary to produce and sustain life. Almost from the beginning, it was infested with organisms. Although numerous these were nothing more than a carpet of single-celled creatures passively absorbing our sun's gifts, unaware and cosmically insignificant. Eventually, more complex life forms appeared and disappeared, victims of a still hostile universe and a constantly changing planetary environment.

About a million years ago a creature appeared which would become modern humans. A creature with a self-awareness sufficient to understand its place in the universe. At first, we told fantastical stories to locate us in the world but as we progressed technologically, we developed tools to probe the furthest reaches of the universe. We could see the furthest stars and we gained a vision of our insignificance in the face of a vast and expanding universe. We could see the smallest particles and we gained an insight into the importance and deep significance of our observations and how they create reality.

The universe took 13.5 billion years to produce a creature with a mind capable of staring into the spaces between the moments of time created by the movement of particles which have existed from the beginning and for which time means nothing. A mind which gives these particles form and which seeks to see past the beginning to understand why there is something rather than nothing and give meaning to an otherwise bleak and unthinking universe.

This mind is also the mind which has planned the traffic system in Swansea City Centre for the past 42 years so I'm going out on a limb here and say we may never find out the meaning of life the universe and everything. Or if we do, we'll build a one-way system around it which will be more difficult to figure out than the actual meaning of life.

Public to plan Swansea City Centre Roads

Swansea is applying for UNESCO World Heritage status for its road layout in the 'legendary impermanence' category.

Swansea City council has launched its interactive traffic planning consultation by revealing the method used to design the road layout for the city centre for the past twenty years. Way ahead of its time, the online tool uses state of the art graphics and a top of the range gaming engine to drive a design platform which has revolutionised the way the road architecture of Swansea has been developed. Based on the ancient sliding puzzle games, examples of which were found in the tomb of Tutankhamun the design package has, for the first time, been thrown open to the public.

Afraid of wide-scale panic at the speed of change to be wrought by the 'Swansea Bay City Deal' a way of maintaining a sense of order and continuity had to be devised. It was decided that, in keeping with tradition, the road layout of Swansea would be redesigned every six months until the 'City Deal' redesign was complete or until the last star faded from the sky, whichever came first. In a bid to encourage participation in the decision-making process the council is holding a competition, the winner of which will get to reconfigure the main thoroughfares across the city.

All you need to do is go onto the council website where you will find the sliding puzzle design tool. Have a play around with it, there's no right or wrong answer as points will be awarded for creativity. When you've finished, submit your design and the one judged to be the most obstructive to both traffic and pedestrians alike, will win. The winner will receive a civic pride achievement award and the honour of seeing their design being the reason the streets of central Swansea are impassable for the next 6 months.

If the competition is a success the council is considering expanding the scheme to include bin collections and school meals.

Swansea City Centre roadworks granted UNESCO world heritage status

Tourists from as far as Australia will flock to see the 'Old World' marvel of a road being celebrated for its totemic rather than practical value.

After losing out to Coventry in the contest to become UK City of Culture 2021, Swansea City Council were understandably devastated but a light has appeared at the end of the tunnel from an unexpected source. The city's ever-changing road layout has made it onto the UNESCO World Heritage List as a cultural site. The surprise ruling comes in the wake of the recent announcement of a scheme to ensure the road works in the city centre never achieve completion.

Dr Kim Il Zeng of the Central University of North Korea will this week publish her PHD on the philosophical and cultural significance of dead road space and the carbon offset advantages of leaving one side of a dual carriagway 'fallow' for several years at a time.

The scheme qualifies for the list under the first three selection criteria. In order to make the list a site needs:

(i) to represent a masterpiece of human creative genius;

The never-ending roadworks concept has been deemed to be a work of counter-intuitive genius by a panel of conceptual artists including Damien Hirst, Damien Hirst's neighbour, (who became a conceptual artist when Damien Hirst said he was) and Marcel Duchamp, who said he would still be an artist after he was dead, so he is.

(ii) to exhibit an important interchange of human values,

over a span of time or within a cultural area of the world, on developments in architecture or technology, monumental arts, town-planning or landscape design;

Town-planning obviously. The interchange of human values over a span of time is demonstrated by the fact that until the concept of never-ending road works was developed people used to think roads were for cars to drive on in order for them to go from one place to another.

(iii) to bear a unique or at least exceptional testimony to a cultural tradition or to a civilization which is living or which has disappeared;

The unique stature of roadworks as an end in themselves is a cultural tradition which exists only in Swansea and which UNESCO has deemed in need of preservation.

Being on the list gives Swansea access to the UNESCO World Heritage Fund which provides about US$4 million annually to support activities requested by States Parties in need of international assistance. It includes compulsory and voluntary contributions from the States Parties, as well as from private donations. This funding should enable Swansea City Council to continue road works well into the next century and beyond, making it a tourist Mecca. The cash injection should also enable it to expand the roadworks outside the city centre, possibly as far as the M4.

Swansea's UNESCO World Heritage Roadworks to be renamed Prince Of Wales Roadworks

A Shaws The Drapers has been on this site since 1192 when it was donated as part of the deal to free Richard I from the clutches of Duke Leopold of Austria.

Her Majesty the Queen and Prime Minister Teresa May have formally agreed the Swansea City Centre roadworks will be officially renamed The Prince of Wales roadworks to commemorate their 60th year without completion.

Welsh Secretary Alun Cairns' temporary, acting, interim junior, non-executive vice-media liaison officer Sean Spicer issued this statement:

"I'm delighted to announce that – with the agreement of the Prime Minister and Her Majesty the Queen – the Swansea City Centre roadworks will be renamed the Prince of Wales Memorial Road Works.

The announcement is a fitting tribute to His Royal Highness in a year that sees him mark 60 years as the Prince of Wales and Swansea's roadworks gaining UNESCO world heritage status. Renaming one of our most iconic landmarks in Wales is a fitting way to formally recognise Prince Charles' commitment and dedication to Wales and the UK as the Prince of Wales."

The ceremony to rename the road works will begin with the convoy of Prince Charles, led by the regalia bearers, entering the Kingsway alternative contraflow, double negative ensemble (with barriers), to await the arrival of Her Majesty.

Once the royal family have arrived, the lesser members will take their seats in the temporary gallery, on the roof of Specsavers. The Queen and Duke of Edinburgh, led by the Earl of Snowdon, the Lord Great Chamberlain, the Earl Marshal and the Gentleman Usher carrying the Great Sword of State, will then make their way to the stage just outside Shaws The Drapers, where the renaming ceremony is to be conducted.

There will then be a short interval of three days as the convoy attempts to decipher the cryptic runes used by city planners to delineate the route through the alternative contraflow, double negative ensemble (with barriers). There will then be another interval of five days as they make their way to the stage.

Spectators are advised that it is perfectly safe and extremely common to drink your own urine when trying to navigate the Kingsway temporary traffic system. Swansea City Council has asked people stuck in the system not to panic as 'all life is transitory and meaning can only be found when we let go of earthly desires like wanting to find the way to Poundstretchers or see your family ever again'.

As he comes to the stage Prince Charles will kneel before the red and white traffic control/anti-terrorist barriers. During the reading of the Letters Patent in Welsh, the Queen will invest Charles with the symbolic Sat Nav, a thermos of hot tea, resident's parking permit, checked blanket and hard boiled sweets, in that order.

Prince Charles will then declare, *"I, Charles, do become your keeper of the mysteries of the one-way system. I dedicate my life to ensuring it shall never be accurately described by any Sat Nav or printed map. Its purpose shall not be revealed, neither by recollection nor legend. Hear this I beseech you; for as long as I live not a man nor woman nor child at the breast will penetrate the arcane wisdom at the heart of the Kingsway lane allocation system. As God is my witness it will ever be thus"*.

Charles will then customarily kiss the Queen's cheek and they will embrace.

The Prince of Wales Memorial Road Works are sponsored by The Crystal Maze.

Carwyn Jones receives Arts Council grant to recreate Swansea's Prince of Wales roadworks

Stage 328 of the Swansea City centre roadworks is directed by Guillermo del Toro and is the much anticipated sequel to his 2006 film Pan's Labyrinth.

The Welsh nation was stunned this week by the news that First Minister the Rt Hon Carwyn Jones AM is to stand down as the leader of Welsh Labour to pursue his artistic ambitions. The Bridgend AM made the surprise announcement in his speech to the Welsh Labour conference in Llandudno where he talked about his obsession with the Prince of Wales roadworks in Swansea.

"I see it as a metaphor, not only for man's inhumanity to man but also for the eternal struggle for meaning in a seemingly

chaotic universe with ever-shifting frames of reference, expanding and contracting timescales and the illusion of purpose in a morally ambiguous landscape. I believe the Prince of Wales roadworks in Swansea is the single greatest work of art we possess today. For something to be art it should have no practical use. It should exist for its own sake and should be resistant to easy or presumptive understanding."

Mr. Jones has been awarded a Creative Professionals grant from the Arts Council of Wales to pursue his interest after leaving office. He intends to use the £30,000 to stage a multimedia performance featuring the roadworks. The purpose is to demonstrate their impact on the national psyche and their specific role as a local agent of disruption.

Over the past thirty years, the roadworks have successfully frustrated generations of shoppers from reaching the centre of Swansea thus, according to one interpretation, achieving their primary purpose of representing the futility of consumer culture in a directionless post cold war Europe. Mr. Jones plans to demonstrate their effectiveness as an agent of disruption by building a life-sized model of them in the middle of the car park of Tesco Extra, Fforestfach.

The measurable outcomes of the artwork will be the drop in till receipts, staff layoffs and angry letters to the editor of the South Wales Evening Post stating that it's the worst thing to happen since they got rid of the Mumbles railway.

The project should secure Swansea's position as the culture capital of Wales for years to come. Swansea City and County Council has moved to trademark the concept of utterly pointless, never-ending roadworks to prevent the Disney Corporation acquiring the rights in a hostile takeover.

Aliens fail to conquer Earth after getting lost in Swansea one way system

Two aliens from the planet Entarpo in the Horse Head Nebular, Fratphompst Nglahagh and Rory Coughdrop gave themselves up to the authorities last week after spending a year and a half attempting to escape the one-way system in Swansea city centre.

Fratphompst and Rory first came to Swansea determined to conquer Wales's second city for the greater glory of the Entarpo Empire, the enrichment of their clan and the triple nectar points with every third off-world conquest. Their plan was to use time honoured Entarpo conquest methods whereby they maximise existing planetary infrastructure. In the case of the Earth, this means roads; upon which they were to unleash the deadly laser-tank to implement a staged annihilation of all civil defenses. Unfortunately, they landed on Oystermouth Road just outside the prison, facing East. Their first instinct was to follow signs for the 'City Centre' where they believed the greatest number of people would be found.

Their disappointment at finding a sparsely populated wasteland resembling Edvard Munch's The Scream but with a Poundstretcher was only exceeded by their rage when they realised they could not find their way back out. Equipped with only enough sandwiches for a thirty-minute conquest they became desperate and pulled over to get a meal deal in the Co-op. A half an hour of queuing later they emerged to see a penalty charge notice on the windscreen of the laser tank which was when they tried to decipher the parking restriction sign next to the vehicle.

Maximum stay 30 minutes, no return within 2 hrs 8am – 6pm Monday to Saturday. Did that mean they could park on a Saturday or to Saturday, meaning Friday but not Saturday? And if they parked at 5:35 did that mean they were OK until the following morning or would they have to leave at 6:05?

They decided to appeal the decision but first, they would leave this barren hell hole for richer pickings. Jumping into the laser tank they soon found they were unable to turn left so took a right only to encounter a row of BFT Stoppy 700 MBB rising bollards.

The Stoppy MBB 230v AC electromechanical bollard with internal oil-bath gear motor is the ideal solution for a range of particular architectural and urban areas with specially designed colours and a new design for the floor flange and light crown. RAL 7015 is the standard finish, they are also available in a stainless steel finish.

Unable to go forward without a smart-card retail environment entry permit the aliens attempted to reverse their way to the complete annihilation of mankind and the eternal glory of the Entarpo Empire. The problem was, a delivery lorry had pulled up behind them and the driver had gone for a coffee. Day one of the planned conquest ended with them eventually pulling into Oxford Street car park to get a bit of rest before launching an all-out attack on day two.

Day two saw them going the wrong way up the Kingsway and finding themselves outside simply pleasure.com where they were at least able to pick up a supply of anal probes which Rory had forgotten to pack. Day three went much the same way as did day four etc. A year and a half later they still hadn't managed to work out which way the traffic was supposed to go on the Kingsway and handed themselves in. By this time they had accrued £67 billion in penalty charges which were enough to pay for the new road layout, Swansea council had always dreamed of.

Schrödinger's road layout will apparently begin construction in three or four years.

Scientists discover evidence of Pre-Christian Roadworks in Swansea City Centre

Before the coming of the Romans or even the Celts, Swansea city centre was being dug up for reasons lost to the mists of time.

Work on the gas pipeline along St. Helens Road in Swansea, has ground to a halt because contractors have unearthed what experts claim to be signs of pre-Christian roadworks. A team of archaeologists from the University of Islamabad have been given six months to investigate the site which could prove to be home to the oldest known road works anywhere in the world.

The roadworks, which are thought to run along St. Helens Road and possibly the entire length of the Kingsway could be up to 5,000 years old and would have most likely been carried out by nomadic tribesmen or early settlers. The current roadworks on the Kingsway have also been put on hold as a precautionary measure.

A spokesman for Swansea Council said *"If a site as ancient and extensive as this proves to be genuine the tourist revenue could be astronomical. Since the road works in the city centre received recognition from UNESCO, Swansea has done a lot to market itself as the pinnacle of chaotic and unfathomable traffic disruption. This could really cement our position on the world stage."*

Although the Prince of Wales Roadworks are known to have dated back some 60 years it is now thought there have been roadworks on the site since the early Bronze age.

Dr. Ahmed Khan of Islamabad University said *"We think this could be linked to the Indus Valley Civilisation which dated from around 3300 to 1300 BC. Although they were originally from Harappa, in the Punjab we know they traveled extensively. I have been pouring over an ancient text which came to light only last year and which I believe demonstrates a link between the Punjab and Wales. The texts are a kind of travelogue and there are constant references to the miserable, relentless rain on almost every page.*

Also in the text is a story about a traveler who is walking along a forest path when he comes across a group of men. The men are standing around talking but beside them is a large hole which they have dug and they will not let him pass. The traveler becomes enraged but they scold him and say it's nothing to do with them. That he should talk to the village elders. So he wanders the forest attempting to find the village elders and he is soon completely lost. Eventually, he is attacked by bears and torn to shreds. His body is never found.

There are many references in this story which I think place it in the Swansea area and the evidence uncovered at the St. Helens Road site seems to support my theory. I believe that roadworks were being carried out in the Swansea area 5,000 years ago and that they greatly inconvenienced locals and travelers alike. We currently have no idea what the exact purpose of the road works was although we are fairly certain they were mostly ceremonial or symbolic, much like today."

German Tourists visit Swansea UNESCO Roadworks

Swansea's Prince Of Wales UNESCO world heritage roadworks are proving a huge success with tourists, we can reveal. This week the MS Amadea which has 620 German passengers on board docked in the city specifically to see the unique cultural phenomenon.

Although it is only on a short two-week cruise around the British Isles, the ship has made the Prince of Wales roadworks a premiere destination. Nowhere else on the planet is it possible to witness roadworks with such a long heritage and diverse set of origin stories.

Germans famously love the British sense of humour and were instantly drawn to this piece of environmental art.

Some say it was the Knights Hospitaller who started them, others traced their origin to the 12th Duke of Beaufort, yet others suggest they could be at least 5,000 years old. Whatever the truth, their strange beauty has caught the eye of the world and Swansea can hold its head up again.

Swansea council's scheme to turn them into a living museum has drawn criticism locally but financially it has been only a massive to crippling burden with almost two tourist boats to date having docked.

A shuttle bus whisked the tourists into the centre of Swansea for ironic shopping opportunities where they were able to see and even touch the roadworks. Soon they were queuing up to take selfies with the hilarious 'Businesses Open As Usual' sign and many of them stood in front of the recently opened 'Roadworks Through The Ages' section with wide-eyed amazement.

Here we see the history of Swansea laid bare. Evidence can clearly be seen supporting the 'out of Africa' theory of human evolution with Cowry Shells having been found in the hardcore substrate.

This section enables visitors to see the stratification of the roadworks as they have been revealed by a team of modern apprentices doing some archaeology. Each inch of roadworks represents 200 years of history and as you reach the bottom you can see the characteristic marks made by flint tools and deer antler pickaxes.

After seeing the roadworks the Germans were taken to the smoking remains of the Amazon fulfillment centre, scene of last months epic battle between juvenile Godzillas, part of Kim Jong Un's plans for world domination and a marauding Orc army created by Swansea council for one purpose. Rather short-sighted as it turns out with Orc unemployment currently running at 100%.

Knights Hospitaller Shady Organisation behind Swansea Roadworks

The history of roadworks in Swansea has been fraught with rancour and shrouded in mystery. Our investigations into the roadworks have shocked us to the core and as a result, we have had to instigate security protocols. I am currently writing this article from a secret location just off the A470. Or am I?

Lewis Weston Dillwyn writing in 1826 described his purchase of 'Longlands' which later became the site of Longlands Hotel. This is currently where the YMCA resides on St. Helens Road. The Eye Wales has discovered that Dillwyn was simply a convenient front for this purchase. The money was put up by an organisation from Lancaster called the Thwait-thorp-dale Mutual Exhumation Society of Friends. Their strangely anachronistic coat of arms appears to feature a ferret performing the Macarena and has recently been revealed to be the ancient Phoenician sign for 'delays possible'.

The symbol fell out of use for thousands of years but was taken up in the 11th century by the order of the Knights Hospitaller because it proved useful when their A&E department was rammed on a Saturday night and it also went with the curtains in their secret lair.

Worlds within worlds, within worlds until we eventually trace the true purchasers of the Longlands property. The most powerful organisation in Medieval Europe and still held by many to be the unseen hand behind the great affairs of the world. Virtually as soon as they had built the Longlands Hotel the Knights Hospitaller began roadworks on St. Helens road. What were they looking for? One hundred and ninety two years later they are still digging and there seems to be no end in sight.

Some say they are after the lost treasure of the temple featuring the ark of the covenant, others that they seek the powers of ancient aliens gifted to early man but lost to the mists of time. There is even a theory that the roadworks themselves are an elaborate ritual wherein the constant digging of trenches and filling in of trenches will eventually release the energies of the underworld making these *the roadworks to end all roadworks*.

We will probably never know exactly why the roadworks in Swansea are never ending but one thing is for sure. The unseen hand of mysterious and malign forces is behind it all and we should dread any power that can cripple a city centre for nearly two hundred years and counting. The truth probably isn't out there.

Swansea Roadworks revealed to be Blitz Themed Folly

In the 18th and 19th century it was a truth universally acknowledged, that a single man in possession of a good fortune, must be in want of an impressive decorative folly for the front lawn. Having done The Grand Tour, marveled at the ruins of Rome and Athens the stinking rich would invariably erect a vision of romantic decay at home to intimidate guests and lend an air of permanence to a newly created landscape garden.

The Georgian and Victorian follies often took the form of decaying abbeys or Hellenistic temples and although nice to look at, were never intended to be used. In a similar vein Henry Somerset, 12th Duke of Beaufort has erected a New Elizabethan folly in the centre of Swansea.

Henry's ancestor 7th Duke of Beaufort won Swansea City centre in a bet and the family has been wondering what to do with it ever since. In 1842 the 7th Duke bet a fellow member of the 'Four-in-Hand Club' that he could navigate the entire British Empire using only a backpack a copy of Whitaker's Astonishing Guide to Native Types and a bottle of smelling salts. Upon his return, he claimed Swansea in what became known as the Gower Peninsular War. Bloodless in all respects it was however considered to be against the Bible's teachings due to Swansea not being mentioned in the Bible.

In the summer of 1973 whilst on a walking holiday in Wales, the 11th Duke decided the landscape of Swansea City centre needed a magnificent ruin to give it a sense of bygone splendor. It already had a run-down castle and a Woolworths so he knew it would have to be something more reminiscent of modern history.

Eventually, he came up with the idea of recreating the blitz. Huge craters, impassible roads and buildings torn down to be replaced by makeshift sheds. Work began in earnest in the 1980s and today we see the completion of the dream. Many people take it to be roadworks and construction which will eventually benefit the people of Swansea in practical terms. It is, in fact, a gigantic folly designed to be best viewed from a townhouse in Belgravia via Google Earth.

Like many follies, its history is little known and its purpose often mistaken for something more practical. This is nothing new in Swansea of course. For a number of years, the County Hall Folly on Oystermouth Road was mistaken by visitors to the area for a fully functional seat of local government.

Live Pac-Man Championships on Swansea Roadworks

Swansea's Prince of Wales UNESCO world heritage roadworks has achieved another coup by attracting the world's first ever live Pac-Man championships to the shores of our lovely second city, we can reveal. The latest stage of the roadworks has seen pedestrians being channeled through an increasingly complex set of barriers designed to test their short-term memory and ability to tolerate enclosed spaces. So far, the barriers have claimed 125 victims with 15 people failing to emerge from minor shopping trips this weekend alone.

Denise Piccolo of Dyfatty told us her friend went missing for five days before eventually being found rummaging through a skip in Penlan.

"She only went in to try out the new launderette and the next thing I know, I'm getting texts and she's telling me she can't remember when she last saw a human face. It was pitiful. There was nothing I could do to help her. Look at this one, see, look...

I don't know where I am Den. How do I find the north star? Is it the big one with the smiley face?

And another one look...

Den, I've just drank my own piss. I'm not being funny but I've had worse pints.

And this next one...

Den, I'm thinking of eating a toe. I don't know where I am. If I set fire to my minge, will the helicopters see it?

It's heartbreaking. And then it all went dead."

Local political satirist Graham Williams has been missing

since last Friday and is feared. He left home in the afternoon carrying a loaf of bread with the intention of dropping a trail of crumbs, secure in the knowledge that seagulls won't go near an olive and quince sourdough batch with a rosemary glaze. He was last seen outside the Halifax trying to ignite a distress flare with his own teeth.

On the plus side, rumours have begun to emerge of a magnificent civilization deep in the heart of the roadworks possessing undreamt of technology and untold mineral wealth, so there's that.

The Pac-Man Live championships will begin in October with Swansea Council leader Rob Stewart scheduled to play the red ghost.

Jackanda Am Byth

In the fading light of a long hot summer night, a man appeared as if from nowhere. He floated above the ground and held his arms wide as if he were welcoming the world. His clothes were like none seen before in Swansea. As he approached people attempting to find their way through the Kingsway roadworks he seemed to beckon. They looked up and followed him for they had been within the roadworks three long hours and were truly without hope. The man took them to a coffee shop that looked like the inside of a shipping container and sold flapjacks made out of Chia seeds and Agave Nectar. They tasted like pure filth. There he sat them down and began his tale.

Long ago, a meteorite struck the sleepy hamlet of Swansea. The town was devastated at first but slowly the people began to use the valuable minerals inside the heaven-sent rock. They mined it for its wealth but soon discovered it contained much more. A substance found nowhere else on Earth, Jackandium, was the source of great power. Using its seemingly endless energy supply the people of Swansea grew strong and made great technological advances. Aware that the rest of the world would covet their great natural advantages they hid themselves behind an increasingly elaborate set of roadworks.

For centuries this protected them from the world. Not one living person knew why the roadworks had been summoned or when they would be completed. Their size and shape was a mystery to even the most advanced cartographers. If they were completed in one area they were just beginning in another. Wave after wave of roadworks turned Swansea into a confusing netherworld of eternally moving cones, railings and bollards. Temporary barriers became permanent before becoming temporary again.

Mysterious paths would appear to channel pedestrians into the heart of darkness. Random lane changes and road layouts would keep drivers in a constant state of confusion, never knowing where to turn or how to reach home. All this deception and obfuscation served one purpose. To hide the location of ancient Swansea, which by now had become 'Jackanda, City of Tomorrow'. The citizens of Jackanda feared that, if their location were revealed they would be destroyed by the jealousy of the wretched without but enough was enough. The devastation they had wrought on outer Swansea became a bone of contention within the Jackandian High Council.

A system of gates was developed allowing the people of Jackanda to pass into outer Swansea to extend help and sustenance to those weary of roadworks and despairing of ever seeing their families again. The gates were to be cleverly hidden behind the comedy 'Businesses Open As Usual' signs. The gates would not only allow Jackandians to pass into outer Swansea but would also enable the people of Swansea to find their way out of the roadworks and reach their loved ones.

A new age of freedom had begun. The roadworks would stay but if the people of Swansea knew where to look and held hope in their hearts they could find a way out, a way to dream and a way to avoid overpriced flapjacks made out of stuff that was good for you.

Swansea Roadworks - The Musical

Swansea City Council in conjunction with Arts Council Wales and The National Theatre of Wales are set to develop a groundbreaking immersive, environmental work of art; 'Swansea Roadworks The Musical'. The search is on for two talented individuals to play star-crossed lovers Tony and Mario. Tony is a slab layer for Sondheim Engineering the company responsible for the interpretive roadworks throughout Swansea whereas Mario is a steel erector for Bernstein Construction Ltd, the builders of the Mi5 regional intrusion office where Martha's Vineyard used to be.

Rivalry

A bitter rivalry between the two crews erupts into violence one Friday night in the Potters Wheel when four men get their thumbs bitten off during a particularly fractious pool tournament. From that day on the men express their mutual hostility by exchanging hard stares across whichever lane of traffic is currently operating on the Kingsway.

Tony and Mario meet when Mario gets stuck up a crane after tea time and Tony, hearing his plaintive cries, scales the outside to bring him a Sweet Onion Chicken Teriyaki on wholemeal with pumpkin seeds. Their romance blossoms but fate is at work driving them apart and Tony is soon forced to choose between his love for Mario and loyalty to the cause of indefinite, interpretive roadworks construction and reconstruction.

Car Park

The musical is scheduled to debut in the car park of Tesco Forest Fach utilising the full-size reconstruction installed by First Minister The Rt Hon Carwyn Jones AM. The book will be written by Virtual Lord Mayor Paul Durden and the score will be written by whoever it is that does all those plinky plonky acoustic covers of rock songs for expensive adverts.

Temporary, acting, interim, vice media liaison officer for Swansea Council Roadworks Creation and Recreation department, Sean Spicer had this to say.

"This is going to be the best musical, all the best notes… The numbers are going to be off the chart for these notes. As, Bs, Ks, everything. All the notes, with words too… It'll be great. We'll have songs, dancing… To the music… With feet. Beautiful feet. All the toes. The best toes. I've seen the music. It just looks great. The most musical… And words too… Big words. But the right ones, not just any words. Great words. Everyone's going to love it.

Any questions?"

Trump ditches Wall in favour of Swansea Roadworks Style Barrier

President Donald Trump has announced he will abandon plans to build a wall across the US Mexican border. Administration officials tasked with delivering on his election pledge to stop illegal immigration have elected to construct a Swansea roadworks style barrier instead. Mr. Trump put his top men on the case as soon as he assumed office with instructions to '*Do whatever it takes*'. Their research led them to Swansea where the roadworks have been successfully preventing people from entering and or leaving the city centre for the past 60 years.

Feral Maze Dwellers

The origin of the roadworks is lost in the mists of time but their efficacy at preventing local businesses from functioning is legendary worldwide. Whether on foot or in a car the roadworks form an impenetrable maze for the unwary and the experienced traveler alike. Their constantly shifting layout and location make it impossible for anyone to navigate them, leading to the development of a population of feral maze dwellers who exist on a diet of Special Brew and discarded seagulls.

Many were born within the roadworks and speak a language of their own. Some of the women stand on street corners, devoid of hope with a glazed expression and only intermediate levels of personal hygiene. A United Nations occupying force, sent into the roadworks last December has been declared missing in action and their families have been notified.

Drug Runners

The efficiency with which the roadworks have destroyed businesses in Swansea over the past 20 years has been an inspiration to the Trump administration. They are convinced a similar layout will have the same detrimental effect on drug runners and people trafficking across the US Mexico border.

Temporary, acting, interim, vice media liaison officer for Swansea Council Roadworks development, exploitation and enmoneyment department, Sean Spicer had this to say.

"My old friend Mr Trump always knew a wall was a big mistake, right from the start. He's never liked walls. He said to me, he said 'impenetrable, never-ending roadworks is the way to go. Anyone can build a wall'. He said it, with his mouth… And teeth. Great teeth. We're going to build him the best God damned roadworks. We'll suck the hope right out of those Mexicans.

*Crushing dreams is what roadworks are all about.
Any questions?"*

Roadworks themed Stained Glass Window for Swansea Market

Plastic barriers

Swansea roadworks enthusiasts have successfully crowd-funded a spectacular stained-glass window to adorn the South facing side of Swansea indoor market we can reveal. The window, which will be a permanent reminder of the permanent roadworks is set to begin construction in the New Year and will feature the now iconic 'BUSINESSES OPEN AS USUAL' road sign obscured by attractive red and white plastic barriers. It will sit directly opposite the Brexit memorial window commissioned by Liberace and will loom over shoppers like an Edgar Allan Poe short story.

Criminals using Google translate

Mr. Karl Emphatic of The Swansea and Lower West Wales Roadworks Enshrinement Society (Sandfields branch) had this to say. *"I sometimes leave the house and can walk for minutes without seeing roadworks. Due to the ever-changing nature of the construction process it is impossible for even the most ardent fan of recreational disruption to predict where they will be. This artwork will give the people of Swansea a focus. A place where they know they will see roadworks whenever they like. It will be an artwork for the people, by the people of the roadworks."*

For economic reasons the window is being manufactured in the Philippines and will be assembled in Swansea by previously nonviolent criminals using Google translate. At night they will be rounded up using an algorithm and Ketamine glue-nets. No problems are anticipated and the completion date is widely believed to be within a human lifespan.

Golden age of roadworks

The window will give hope to the people of Swansea, many of whom don't believe the current golden age of roadworks can last much longer. Although Swansea council has given assurances that the now world-famous UNESCO Prince of Wales roadworks will not be going anywhere rumours are rife of secret plans to render city centre roads 'usable'.

Whatever the outcome of the actual roadworks, Swansea will soon have a piece of public art to rival the ceiling of the Sistine Chapel in its scope and thematic grandeur. Or something like that.

Swansea Roadworks Festival to rival Glastonbury

Swansea Council has agreed a deal with Glastonbury overlord Michael Eavis to alternate years between the world-renowned festival and a celebration of all roadworks related activities. The Glastonbury trust, an offshoot of the Michael Eavis bathroom and novelty porridge empire is in talks with city leaders in a bid to extend the 'fallow years' to a biannual event. The fallow years normally occur every five years to give the land, local population, and organisers a break but with an alternative venue, the Glastonbury spirit can be kept alive artificially.

Feral roadworks residents

Shops across the city have already begun developing window displays in anticipation of feeling the mighty festival's corporate thud. In keeping with original hippy ideals, the festival will be entirely free. However, there will be a nominal charge of £50 per day for parking and people bringing their own food into the city centre will be tasered and returned to the wild. The festival is expected to attract tens of people, many of whom will bring tales of the outside world.

Feral residents of the road works will receive a discount of £1.50 a day off parking; £2.50 if they own a vehicle.

Beyonce to headline

Beyonce and Jay-Z will headline on Saturday night just in front of the big screen in Castle Square. They will wow crowds with all their roadworks related hits such as Single Laneys and 99 Problems (but a ditch ain't one). Those puns were officially sanctioned by the post-Brexit committee for taking back control of fun. They have been deemed funny by a panel of experts who know a good joke when they hear it. The panel's other duties include taking back control of knees-ups and beer temperatures.

The roadworks festival will culminate in a parade through the streets which is expected to last until the end of recorded time or until Britain leaves the European Union, whichever is longer. The BBC has secured the broadcast rights for the festival but will be covering it from a safe distance offshore. They will use drones for the filming in a technique they call 'using drones'. Since losing fifteen journalists, sent to cover Santa's parade last November, the BBC have been forbidden by their insurance company from sending any employees anywhere near the 'gravitational pull' of the roadworks themselves.

Santa makes Swansea Roadworks look bad

The peerless reputation of Swansea's UNESCO world heritage Prince of Wales roadworks has been tarnished this year by a lacklustre Christmas parade and local councillors have sworn to 'wreak terrible vengeance on Santa and all his stunted minions'. Swansea council has been trying to summon up the true spirit of Christmas all year round by generating a hemmed-in feeling of claustrophobia throughout the whole of the city centre via the use of conceptual roadworks and regular mid-morning drunken tableaux. Unfortunately, Father Christmas refused to do his bit to continue the theme resulting in angry mobs armed with flaming torches and pitchforks descending on council buildings.

Full blown diplomatic incident

The Christmas parade featuring Santa Clause and his elves normally brings great joy to city dwellers but this year a trademark dispute over the colours red and white threatened to derail the event completely. What began in February as a polite exchange of emails wherein Santa jokingly suggested the colour scheme of the roadworks would make it difficult for people to see him, gradually escalated into a full-blown diplomatic incident. By June the Lapland ambassador wrote to the United Nations after learning the roadworks would still be in place during Santa's scheduled parade in November 2018, 2019, 2020, 2021 etc.

After this, Santa himself cut off all contact with Swansea council and would only respond through his solicitors. Via a series of official emails Felcher, Spitroast and Updyke made Swansea council aware that their client would honour his commitment to 'parade through the streets like a ten-cent whore, waving at hysterical vermin, glorifying the consumerist theocracy' but he would not bring any of the usual 'good cheer' or 'Christmas magic'.

Prevent unskilled elves working

The council responded with an open letter in the Guardian stating they were going to 'take back control of Christmas' and would be introducing a points-based system to prevent unskilled elves working within the city. Santa himself could no longer expect to go to the front of the queue if he wanted to enter the city but would have to demonstrate that he would not be a burden on the local economy. He would also not be allowed to access the benefits system nor avail himself of NHS or education services.

Cheap wine and fifteen Thorazine

Unable to extricate himself from his legal duty to 'parade', Santa turned up on the 18th of November in a massive sulk having consumed three bottles of cheap wine and fifteen Thorazine. By 2pm he had punched three reindeers and urinated over a toddler named Flint. By 5pm, as contracted, he climbed aboard his sleigh and headed off through the city centre only partially conscious. From there it went downhill fast and complaints poured in on social media, mostly about the clash of colours between the roadworks and Santa's costume.

On Monday the 19th of November Swansea councilors wrote another open letter to the Guardian stating Santa had brought the city centre roadworks into disrepute and that they would hunt him down and terminate him with extreme prejudice. His head would be mounted on a spike in front of the Guild Hall and an avenue of burning elves would light the way of next year's Christmas parade. Or he could always change to a green outfit with gold trim, whatever.

Swansea Council to start charging people to leave the Roadworks

In a surprise move, Swansea City council has purchased the toll booths from the recently liberated 'Prince of Wales Bridge' in an attempt to monetize the UNESCO world heritage roadworks.

The Prince of Wales interpretive roadworks, which celebrated their 61st-year last summer, have drawn millions of tourists but upkeep is becoming expensive. Many schemes have been hatched over the years to try to develop a sustainable model for the much-loved roadworks. At one point the cash-strapped council sold shares and it was a year before they realised 'so-called ISIS' had bought a controlling interest in the Kingsway temporary utility roundabout. They had been using it for terrorist purposes for six months before anybody noticed.

Dick Springfield of Dunvant was livid. *"They had been using it for the terrorism. Roundabout terrorism is one of the worst kinds you can have and they was doing it all the time as it turned out. Their technique was to slightly improve congestion in the immediate vicinity of the roundabout using a series of controlled explosions and YouTube rants with masks on. The knock-on effect gridlocked the rest of the city centre for three days. What people don't understand is what a finely balanced ecosystem the roadworks are. These terrorists will stop at nothing, up to and including stopping anything and everything that moves in the city centre."*

Unable to finish even a simple pavement Swansea Council are having to raise funds for more roadworks.

The toll booths will be installed on the Kingsway and people will be charged £15.85 to leave the roadworks system, £32.67 if they have children in the vehicle. Money raised will be used to fund the continuation of the roadworks on the Kingsway.

Council leader Rob Stewart stated that: *"Without the toll booths, there is a very real danger the roadworks will become financially unsustainable by the end of 2019. I understand that members of the public will object to the cost of leaving our, in many ways, groundbreaking conceptual traffic dilemma but what I would ask them to consider is just how much they want to see their loved ones again and how much they are prepared to pay."*

Temporary, acting, interim, vice media liaison officer for Swansea Council Roadworks development, exploitation and enmoneyment department, Sean Spicer had this to say.

"Yeah man. It was like we were in a dream and they were coming out of the sky like giant bats and they covered the cars in big bat dandruff. We were screaming and screaming and all of our lips were made of turquoise and vanilla but the bad man used it to... Sorry, what was the question?"

With fifty thousand people a month becoming lost in the roadworks system the toll booths are expected to raise over £15 million a year. The restaurant chain Subway has launched a legal challenge insisting that people being able to leave the city centre will hit their passing trade. As a result, they have been granted a five-year rates rebate and a temporary license to harpoon people out of their cars on quiet days.

Banksy Artwork found in Swansea Roadworks

World famous graffiti artist Banksy has confirmed his latest creation is on the side of a concrete barrier in the middle of Swansea's UNCRC world heritage Prince of Wales roadworks.

The artwork appeared on the barrier at the eastern end of the Kingsway in the city centre over the weekend.

It covers half a barrier with a picture of the legendary Minotaur of Greek legend who famously dwelled within the Labyrinth. The Minotaur is shown consulting a Sat Nav device in a desperate attempt to find his way out of Swansea city centre.

Toothbrush and a lottery ticket

The work had sparked wild speculation that it could be a Banksy after images began circulating on social media.

But confirmation only came today when Banksy issued this statement. *"After I did that one up in Port Talbot, I thought I'd pop into Swansea to do a bit of shopping.*

Swansea city centre is famous for its 'ironic_shopping' and the council has even commissioned a massive stained glass window to celebrate the fact.

I needed some toilet roll and, a new toothbrush and a lottery ticket for the triple rollover. Three and a half hours later I still hadn't managed to find anywhere to park."

Harpooned by Subway staff

Even though I hadn't succeeded in parking my car I'd been given three parking tickets filled out a shopping experience consumer satisfaction survey and been harpooned out of my car by staff from the Subway on Union Street. The sweet onion chicken teriyaki on wholemeal with pumpkin seeds was delicious as it happens but the harpoon wound still hasn't healed and I'm on antibiotics which have effectively destroyed my digestive system, so swings and roundabouts.

After my sandwich, I came out and saw the concrete barriers. Well, I thought, while I'm here I might as well knock up one of my famous cutting edge, anti-establishment, socio-political, satirical artworks using my legendary graffiti skills. Bish, bash, bosh, ten minutes later there it is. I call it Minor Tour (with Sat Nav). It's like a play on words see?

Dipping Sauce

Anyway, if anyone has seen my car, I'd appreciate it if you could let me know. It's a 1992 pearlized green and silver Fiat Panda with rear spoilers and there's a pizza on the back seat with three slices left. Spicy beef with extra cheese and olives. And a Garlic Parmesan White dipping sauce. And a large Coke. That's not important but you know..."

The Banksy is estimated to be worth in excess of £300,000 or something like that. Swansea council has vowed to 'Power wash it out of existence' as soon as any of their cleaning units can work out how to find their way from The Quadrant to The Kingsway without getting a parking ticket.

Swansea Council wash £300,000 Banksy off Roadworks

Swansea Council has power washed their Banksy out of existence and hope it will be a lesson to others that this sort of behaviour simply won't be tolerated.

Eagle-eyed readers will remember a Banksy artwork suddenly appeared in the depths of the Prince of Wales Roadworks last week. This week I can report it has been successfully cleaned up using a mixture of environmentally friendly facial bleaching technology, good old-fashioned elbow grease and the Hyundai P1PE P4200PWT Petrol Pressure Washer. But mostly the pressure washer.

Sleep deprivation and motivational emptiness

Upon learning there was a Banksy defacing the roadworks, Swansea council immediately authorised the use of all necessary force to ensure its removal. A crack cleaning team was dispatched, probably from that weird bit between the Market and the Quadrant shopping centre or somewhere like that, to erase the offending graffiti. They set out on Monday evening and by Wednesday had reached the new, temporary looking roundabout at the western end of the Kingsway.

Suffering from sleep deprivation and motivational emptiness they sent up a distress flare which luckily caught the eye of the coast guard.

Since the latest phase of the Prince of Wales Roadworks began plain clothes coast guard officers have started patrolling the city centre offering navigational tips, astrolabes and basic rations to stranded motorists and pedestrians. It is estimated they have reduced roadworks related dystopian fiction by 83% and rumour has it, one person made it out of the city centre and has been reunited with their family.

Royal Edinburgh Military Tattoo

With the help of the coast guard, the cleaning team were able to travel the 500 yards to the other end of the Kingsway within four short days and like a team of sailors at the Royal Edinburgh Military Tattoo they unloaded their cleaning equipment and set to work.

Cleaned its ass

Lickety-split the graffiti was gone and the streets were restored to their pristine pre-art state. Temporary, acting, interim, vice media liaison officer for Swansea Council Roadworks uglification avoidance department, Sean Spicer had this to say.

"Yeah, we cleaned it. We cleaned its ass. We cleaned it good.

Yeah... Coming into my town... My town... My town and with graffiti. My town... This is the line in the sand. You graffiti in my town and it will be cleaned. We got the best cleaners. Cleaners like you've never... Like you've never seen... You'll see. We made these roadworks great again and we'll do it again. I say this to Banksy, you will not do art on these great roadworks. We're all proud of these roadworks. We built roadworks to last a thousand years and as God is my witness you will not tarnish that vision. I will hunt you down and kill you myself with my fingers.

Any questions?"

The News II

Westminster Cabinet Members to be issued with Red Shirts

Prime Minister Theresa May has announced a new dress code for her cabinet. From now on ministers will simply be issued with red shirts, we can reveal. The 'Red Shirt' policy is thought to have been inspired by the science fiction TV series 'Star Trek' where crew members wearing red shirts invariably come to a violent end, usually brought on by their own stupidity or treachery.

The red shirt will be a tight-fitting sweat-shirt style garment designed to restrict freedom-of-movement but more importantly, it will hide blood spatters should any cabinet member shoot themselves in the foot or decide to stab another cabinet member in the back. The exception to the rule will be The Minister of State for Northern Ireland as members of Sinn Féin have refused to meet with anyone even vaguely orange. The DUP, however, have told the Prime Minister in private they will not countenance any separate dress code for Northern Ireland.

The red shirt policy appears to be extremely unpopular amongst backbenchers as well with many saying the Prime Minister should deliver the dress code the people voted for. This is thought to refer to David Cameron's 2010 election pledge to 'Hug a hoodie'. The powerful 'Dressing In Commons Committee' (DICC) has been pushing for the hoodie to be adopted across the Houses of Parliament and it's chair has stated publicly he is prepared for a no clothes scenario where MPs turn up as God intended but in most case, slightly fatter.

With no resolution in sight, the government has issued instructions on how to prepare if MPs turn up in parliament with no clothes. The importing and exporting animal products section has some very specific recommendations regarding sanitation whereas the rules on 'trading gas' remain largely unaffected. As yet there have been no preparations for a hung parliament. The no clothes instructions contain the following assurance.

"People and businesses should not be alarmed by 'no clothes' planning and preparation, nor read into it any pessimism. Instead, they should be reassured that we are taking a responsible approach, ensuring the 'Red Shirt' dress code transition can be as smooth as possible in all scenarios."

Secret fracking in Tenby

The history of fracking has been checkered, to say the least. Tales of contaminated water supplies and earthquakes abound but none can be as strange as the Tenby connection. In 1860 Josiah Reginald Steppewad Coldstrap, Mr Coldstap to his friends, devised a method of extracting gas from shale which was identical to modern day fracking in every respect.

The south west of Wales holds rich deposits of 'unconventional gas' along its coastline and Tenby sits at the epicentre of a massive field. The Victorians, great innovators that they were, knew this but had no means of extracting it. Josiah Coldstrap had not only a dream but a revolutionary device which he said would release the untold riches. He petitioned the Queen for permission to drill and a modicum of finance to sustain him in his endeavours. Her Majesty gave him short shrift but Albert Prince Consort was fascinated by the idea.

Behind Victoria's back, he bankrolled the venture and cleared the necessary permits. So excited was he by the venture he journeyed to Tenby to help with the work himself. Drilling started on the 2nd of February 1861. By the 15th they had hit gas and in a cruel twist of fate had killed Prince Albert outright. Forced out by the pressure of gas, a retardant flange piston caught him under his left arm stopping his heart immediately.

Such was the anticipated scandal (a member of the royal family performing manual labour) that the official story had him dying of the then popular 'vitals disease', Typhoid. The venture was shut down and the drilling rig, too big to be moved was covered over with a massive plinth. So massive in fact was the plinth that it dwarfed the subsequent statue of the Prince Consort erected by the citizens of Tenby, to a man who had become a great friend in a short space of time.

Cop show Manic, Street and Preacher on ITV hailed as the new Breaking Bad

Reaction to new ITV drama 'Manic, Street and Preacher' has been mixed with some people calling it the new Breaking Bad and others reporting boredom induced fitting. The buddy, cop drama is about three ex-Metropolitan police officers who initially don't do things by the book and because of this get very poor results. In the first episode, they are sent to a small rural community to solve a series of grisly tanning salon licensing issues relating to non-EU regulation breaker switches.

There they slowly learn to read the beauty and self-enhancement European licensing regulatory rulebook, then they not only to do things by it but they also to teach others how to do so. Producer Marshall Schlom compared it to Homer's Odyssey in that the heroes grow emotionally throughout the series and eventually embark on teaching careers where they show police cadets the importance of following rules because of the massively increased rate of convictions such an approach results in.

They also point to the soft benefits of better community relations and enhanced public trust due to a sense of greater accountability.

A spin-off from the much-acclaimed reality show 'If You Tolerate This Then You'll Love Strictly Come Dancing', the program features three unknown actors who were chosen because they said they could bring their own suits. Sean Moore, James Dean Bradfield and Nicky Wire all graduated from the Rhyl Academy of Dramatic Art; beneficiaries of the Kim Jong Un scholarship program. The series has taken the internet by storm and has been lauded as a high-water mark in the current 'Golden Age of Television'.

Hailed as the first ever police series where the central protagonists do things by the book the format has allowed the writers to explore complex issues of delayed gratification and maintaining a personal moral framework within a wider and seemingly impersonal system designed to express and impose societal norms of compassion and fairness via a top-down authoritative structure. Also in episode three 'Street' falls asleep inside a tanning bed and pisses himself, with hilarious results.

The Disney Corporation has bought the world rights as a precautionary measure. *'Manic, Street and Preacher'* is on ITV and is sponsored by Greggs.

Wales renamed Prince of Wales Land

Wales has been renamed Prince of Wales Land in a bold move by Secretary of State for Wales Alan Cairns as he bids to steal American tourists from the increasingly popular Gaza Strip.

Tourism along the strip has sky-rocketed in the last year due to end-of-days package tours. The Gaza Strip has been identified, by Trump family friend and Astrologer Des O'Connor, as the place where the final battle will be fought between the forces of good and evil.

It was O'Connor who first predicted the Trump win in 2016 and O'Connor again who saw the writing on the wall with regard to two for one offers on multi-packs of ridge cut crisps in Tesco Metros. The final battle, featuring the destruction of all life on earth will of course usher in the return of the Messiah and the ascent into heaven of God's chosen ones. Yes, that includes Donald Trump, why wouldn't it? American fundamental Christians wanting a ringside seat are flooding into the Gaza Strip armed with popcorn, La-Z-Boy reclining chairs and of course, guns.

Tempting them and their Dollars over to Wales has long been the ambition of ambitious Secretary of State for Wales Alan Cairns. Unable to manufacture a perpetual state of local conflict that threatens to engulf the entire world in nuclear Armageddon Mr. Cairns has gone for the next best thing; Royal Warrant status.

For years now Prince Charles has wanted a small country to put in the back garden of the Duchy of Cornwall and it looks like he has finally got his way. Using all his political cunning and with an unerring instinct for what the people of Wales want the Secretary of State handed the entire country over to the prince and renamed it into the bargain. Mr. Cairns has been awarded a knighthood and a lifetime supply of Tesco's ridge cut crisps, which because of the offer is actually two lifetimes supply. A spokesman for Mr. Cairns said he will be donating the other lifetime's supply to raise money for The Obesity Health Alliance.

Due to Prince Charles's famous love of organic farming methods, part of the deal will entitle the Duchy of Cornwall to collect the urine of every man, woman and child in Prince of Wales Land and transport it over the Prince of Wales bridge to be used as fertilizer on the lemon shortbread plantations.

Temporary, acting, interim, vice media liaison officer for The Office of the Secretary of State for Wales, Sean Spicer had this to say.

I'm not saying force will be used. It won't... Almost none. It's up to you. If you want to tug your forelock, you can. It's a beautiful thing. A deferential thing. You know just a little... I'm not saying really yank it, you know. A lot of people don't have forelocks these days. Older people... Older men... You can doff your cap or do a bow. And we can have bowing lessons. For the tourists. It'll look better. They have certain expectations and we'll need a national anthem they can actually sing, with words in English so...

Any questions?

The Welsh Space Program

A Welsh space program is something I've been interested in for years. Back in the 1990s I wrote a screenplay featuring and old man who was building an orbital rocket in his back yard so when the idea of Llanbedr being used as a launch site hit the headlines, I was very excited.

It was a short journey then to combine it with the Trump/Liberace dichotomy as well as mundanities of the Welsh government's vision for economic regeneration. I love thinking about the comical practicalities of grand projects and it occurs to me that in order to make space exploration self-funding, it is at some point going to have to be opened up to actual people. What could possibly go wrong?

Space Force to rule the heavens from Llanbedr

Llanbedr in North Wales is set to become the centre of Liberace's new 'Space Force'. The world-renown pianist has vowed to make orbital caravan holidays available 'to the hoi polloi'. When it was first announced it on Twitter most people imagined the Space Force would be used for military purposes but as usual, Liberace sees the bigger picture. Tow bars will be fitted to all shuttles leaving from Llanbedr. Inflight entertainment will be provided either by The Krankies or awkward silences interspersed uncomfortable shuffling and arguments over charging points.

In a survey of a thousand residents of Llanbedr in 2017, 80% expressed a reluctance to venture into space with most citing the lack of kitchen facilities and having to learn another language as the main deterrents. Having spent many a memorable summer in Fishguard in his static caravan, Liberace realised the mobile home was the obvious solution to almost all space exploration issues.

Llanbedr airfield was shortlisted as a location for a UK spaceport by the Government in 2015. In 2016 the Government scrapped the competition to choose a site and instead invited locations to apply for a license. Llanbedr town council believe they are the front-runners because none of the other locations have tow bars on their shuttles or any kind of family entertainment. Two of them don't even provide free bed linen and one doesn't allow dogs in space.

Initial fears by local campsite owners that they would lose valuable land to the spaceport have been alleviated by the offer of shares in the venture and the promise of control of the Londis franchise. At a press conference, last Tuesday temporary, interim, acting, caretaker media liaison janitor Sean Spicer had this to say.

"The caravan space force will be the best space force there is. Fitted kitchens... Fitted. With all the best, everything. You'll see... This will make other space caravan parks look like little, tiny, itty bitty... This is going to be the Glastonbury of space caravan parks. We've already got Jane McDonald booked for Tuesday evenings. Bingo on Mondays and Thursdays. Wednesday is Karaoke night in the Trump Lounge and on Saturday nights Liberace himself will be playing a medley from the great American songbook and Stock Aitken Waterman greatest hits between lunch and tea-time.

Sunday will be inter caravan Mixed Martial Arts tournaments and we also make quite a big thing of sewage disposal. I don't know if you've ever seen a three hundred kilo turd re-entering the earth's atmosphere but it's quite the cause for celebration, I can tell you.

Any questions?"

Donald Trump's Space Force, renamed 'Prince of Wales Force'.

Secretary of State for Wales Alan Cairns has outdone himself this week by unilaterally renaming Donald Trump's Space Force, 'Prince of Wales Force' we can reveal. The Space force calls for the Pentagon to develop a sixth branch of the American armed services that would protect national and commercial interests in space. 'Prince of Wales Force' will do the same but will also use zero gravity laboratories to develop a thinner, crisper Duchy Original Organic Sicilian lemon all butter shortbread.

A major plank of the 'Prince of Wales Force' will be a sustainable return to the Moon and Llanbedr in North Wales will be the hub of the Moonbase Alfa development scheme. Thanks to their experience in designing off world static caravan parks Llanbedr town council have been asked to lead the ambitious first stage in 'conquering the known universe'. Quick off the mark, they have already begun towing fifteen Atlas Mirage Deluxe Caravans into orbit around Earth's nearest neighbour.

This time next year they should have all necessary amenities installed but they are still in talks with the Pentagon regarding the price of a unit. Llanbedr Council insist they can provide the caravans for $1.5M each.

Price Includes:
- 2018 standard pitch fees
- Siting, pre-delivery inspection and anchors
- Connections for gas, electricity and water
- Axel Jacks
- Fire extinguisher, carbon monoxide detector and smoke alarm
- Ramtech alarm

- Steps and handrails
- Digital TV aerial
- Fridge

The Pentagon have requested triple lead-lined bunker strength exterior cladding, assassin droids patrolling the perimeter and tea making facilities. President Trump has personally requested Bingo in the mess hall on alternate Wednesdays. When he visits the base in 2019 Mr. Trump will be the first sitting President to visit the Moon since Theodore Roosevelt in 1908.

Teddy Roosevelt was the first American in space. In those days all you needed was a can-do attitude and enough space in your plus fours for a Thermos of Bovril.

Mr. Roosevelt, accompanied by child actor Lionel Jeffries planted the American flag on the moon during a mission which saw them frustrate the plans of a race of giant insect men intent of destroying The Earth using assassin droids and tea making facilities. When will we ever learn?

Wales to launch Convention Centre into Space

The First Minister for Wales the Rt Hon Carwyn Jones AM looked at his hands and wondered. 'Are these the hands of a great man'? Would he be remembered as someone who took Wales by the scruff of the neck and dragged it into the twenty-first century or would his legacy fade like a rugby player's fake tan? Did he really have what it takes to make Wales great again? And should he get a manicure before the interview or didn't it really matter for radio?

The interview would be his parting shot in the general direction of immortality. A low-key announcement he knew would reverberate around the world. He would create a Space Force and it would rule the heavens between St Davids and Chepstow. Also, up the north as well. It would be called the Celtic Manor, RBS Group Space Resort/Force. Its main purpose would be to rule the heavens with an iron fist. Its secondary purpose would be to capitalise on the work done by Llanbedr Council with their revolutionary space caravan park to launch the world's first fully bilingual space conference centre.

Anyone working for a national organisation in Wales is aware of the need for a conference centre which is equally inconvenient for absolutely everyone. Llandrindod Wells has previously cornered the market in such venues because of its central location just off the A470 but for many purists, it's simply not inconvenient enough.

A space conference centre which can be reached from spaceports in Llanbedr, North Wales and the Black Rock picnic site located between the Severn bridge and The Prince of Wales bridge was the perfect solution. The space conference centre, when completed would accommodate up to 5,000 delegates. The venue would include a 4,000sqm pillar-free main hall, a 1,500-seated auditorium, 12 flexible meeting rooms, a double-height glass atrium and a 2,500 sqm outdoor plaza.

Artists impression of what the space conference centre would look like if it wasn't in space.

As he looked in the mirror and dared to dream Carwyn Jones imagined a world where patrons would be advised that the left-hand side of the outdoor plaza had been designated a non-smoking area. He dared to dream of a Wales that ruled the heavens immediately above Wales with an iron fist using advanced technology to do ruling. Anyone who dared challenge the might of Wales in that geographically specific area would feel the wrath of its people in some way or other, involving space stuff.

Llanbedr spaceport will shuttle millions of people a year up to the space conference centre where they will be met with a trolley featuring Custard Creams, Bourbons, Chocolate Digestives and Digestives along with flapjacks with fruit in them and maybe a Bakewell tart. There will also be coffee, tea and a selection of herbal teas, one of which will involve nettles.

The first event to take place there would be the 2019 UK Space Conference. All the pieces were falling into place and Carwyn knew the one man who could deliver the project on budget and on time. The one man who could bring to bear the combined skills of Earth's mightiest heroes.

That man was Vampire Elvis.

Vampire Elvis

Since the death of Elvis Presley on August 16, 1977, rumours about a conspiracy have persisted. The conspiracy goes like this. Elvis faked his own death and entered a witness protection program because on August 15, 1977, he gave evidence against a criminal organisation known as 'The Fraternity'. This, of course, is nonsense. The fact of the matter is, he faked his own death because he became a vampire as part of a fad diet. The diet didn't work.

For years after his 'death' Elvis remained underground. He found being 'dead' gave him greater freedom to pursue his favourite pastime of fighting crime. At first, he was tackling things like bank robberies and muggings on an ad-hoc basis using the time honoured superhero method of lurk and pounce. He wore a mask for two reasons. The first to conceal the fact that he was Elvis; after all, he was undercover. The second was that if the mask was dislodged during a fight, his enemy would be so staggered that they were being beaten up by Elvis they would lose their composure and fall prey to his sneaky pincer move.

Unfortunately, after a while, he realised he wasn't actually doing much good. The problem was all down to numbers. Being a vampire, he could only fight crime at night. This ruled out at least 50% of all crime. The other thing was that, on a good night, he could capture/beat up about five or six criminals. That would average out at about 2,000 crimes a year whereas the total number in America alone is close to 14,000,000. Eventually, he decided he needed to get tough on the causes of crime.

He journeyed to Washington DC and infiltrated, first the FBI, then the department of justice and even the Executive Office of the president. Each time he came across the same problem. The issue was just too big; too complex. There was no cause of crime. It turned out to be a many-layered problem of social and economic inequality, urban neglect, rural neglect, over criminalisation of specific activities, substance misuse, societal attitudes, and any number of other factors relating to education, healthcare, readily available firearms and rampant, free-market consumerism. That doesn't even begin to take into account the fact that some people are just horrible.

After years of getting nowhere, he resolved to move to somewhere more manageable. A smaller or more law-abiding country. At first, he went to Canada. This seemed to have less crime but it was still way too big a problem to be solved by one man randomly beating up street criminals. Again he entered the system of government; again he grew disillusioned with the prospect of ever changing anything. He decided to downsize even more.

Three years later he ended up in Iceland, a country with a population of barely more than 300,000. Here he felt he could make a difference. Besides which, it was dark for most of the year, which meant he could take up jogging and finally shed those extra pounds.

Unfortunately even Iceland proved too tricky and complex a problem for a, by now, thoroughly dejected Vampire Elvis. Moving on from Iceland he searched and searched the world for a country small and simple enough to be the place where he could make a difference. After failing to master the social complexities of the Pitcairn Islands he eventually moved to Wales where he was given a ministerial position without portfolio.

For months he haunted the corridors of power, eager to do his bit to fight crime until one day in December 2013, First Minister the Rt Hon Carwyn Jones AM placed a paternal hand on his shoulder and took him to meet The Standard Spending Assessment and New innovation fund

Communities First Avengers (SSANIFCFA for short).

It was to prove a fateful day for all concerned.

If the Corridors of Power could talk

Vampire Elvis, Minister Without Portfolio, strolled nonchalantly through the corridors of power as if he owned them. He had recently been strolling through the corridors of empowerment. These were a new initiative from the Communities and Tackling Poverty portfolio which mainly consisted of making the ceilings of the corridors of power slightly lower so Welsh people could feel taller. This would give them a sense of empowerment, leading to statistically greater levels of overall achievement during their careers.

Vampire Elvis had hit his head three times in the first four minutes and was trying to find his way around the Welsh Assembly using only the corridors of power. There were now so few actual corridors of power that he did indeed feel like he owned them. A hand suddenly snaked out from a doorway, grabbed him by the collar and yanked him into an office.

First Minister the Rt Hon Carwyn Jones AM pinned him up against a wall and glanced at the door like a cornered animal. His foot flew out and kicked the door closed.

VAMPIRE ELVIS

Uh, hu, I er…… I just think of you as a friend man….

Well, more like an acquaintance actually….

CARWYN

No, don't be stupid mun. I've got it. I know what it's all about.

VAMPIRE ELVIS

Uh hu…

CARWYN

A Welsh Space Force.

VAMPIRE ELVIS

Uh hu….

CARWYN

When it comes to protecting our nation and our
way of life, the only thing we can't afford is inaction.

VAMPIRE ELVIS

I'm with you there baby.

CARWYN

The Welsh people deserve our very best and they will have it.
It is not enough merely to have a Welsh convention centre in
space, we must have Welsh dominance in space.

VAMPIRE ELVIS

Uh, hu….

CARWYN

Previous administrations all but neglected the growing

security threats emerging in space. Space is a
warfighting domain just like land and air and sea.
The Welsh Space Force will strengthen our security,
it will ensure our prosperity.

VAMPIRE ELVIS
You're crumpling my shirt man.

CARWYN
It will also carry Welsh ideals into the boundless expanse
of space. While other nations increasingly possess
the capability to operate in space, not all of them
share our commitment to freedom, private property
and the rule of law.

VAMPIRE ELVIS
God damn it, that's what I've been saying.

CARWYN
So, as we continue to carry Welsh leadership in
space so also will we carry Wales's commitment
to freedom into this new... Final frontier.

VAMPIRE ELVIS
So.........

CARWYN

So, we need to put the team back together.

The Space Force must happen.

Welsh Space Force Logo: The Reviews are in

Our dear leader has taken the first important step toward Welsh dominance of space. The First Minister for Wales the Rt Hon Carwyn Jones AM has unveiled the new logo for the Welsh Space Force and the reviews are in. The logo which is loosely based on one of the prospective American Space Force logos features the Welsh dragon striking a dynamic pose as it shoots up into space.

The exact cost of the logo development process is not known but is thought to be in the region of £600,000 as this was the amount of underspend left in the budget of the statutory committee for monitoring departmental underspend.

A freedom of information request revealed the statutory committee for monitoring departmental overspend requested the money to plug a hole in its finances but was refused after an ironic intervention by the committee for ironic interventions. One of the conditions for the logo was that it would have to reproduce well when shone against clouds via a powerful searchlight.

The chair of the committee for carrying Welsh ideals into the boundless expanse of space issued a statement revealing that this would be the chief method of summoning The Space Force when the nation was in peril or something.

Reviews have been entirely negative with celebrity, celebrity Peter Andre describing it as "*a bit like in a shop, when someone on the checkout is trying to get you to sign up to a loyalty card but you don't fully realise what's happening so you have to ask them to explain it again because you weren't really paying attention and then you don't understand the points system and you try to work out how much you'll have to spend before you get anything back and then you realise you haven't been in the shop for over a year so you'll probably never use it anyway. A bit like that but with Logos".*

The reviews of his review were mostly negative with @reviewingreviews saying *"I literally have no idea what he's talking about. I don't think he fully or even partially understands the concept of a review".*

Regardless of the unambiguously hostile reception for the logo, Our Dear Leader will be pressing on with this first stage in the conquest of space. Stage two, the choosing of the font for press releases, will begin in earnest after the summer recess.

Other books from articles first published in the Eye eMagazine published by Cambria Publishing in paperback and eBook format.

Visit the website at
https://www.cambriabooks.co.uk/product/a-good-story/